A HERITAGE OF DEATH

A REVEREND CICI GURULE MYSTERY

BOOK 2

ALEXA PADGETT

A Heritage of Death © 2018 Alexa Padgett

ISBN-13: 978-1-945090-23-3

Edited by Deborah Nemeth and Nicole Pomeroy
Cover Art by Emma Rider of Moonstruck Cover Design & Photography

For Tracey

Tracey—

Thank you for all
the wonderful walks!

Olivia Padgett

1

Cici

Our earthly joys are almost without exception the
creatures of a moment… — Rousseau

A text from a blocked number read: If you want to see your baby
again come out to Service Road 705. There's a cabin at the very end.

She found the ramshackle but serviceable structure. She didn't
enter. Behind it about an eighth of a mile was the root cellar. That's
where she was now—where he'd brought Isabel earlier.

She hadn't seen him when she came in, but he must have been
lurking in the thick shadows.

"Hello, Grace," he said, his voice smug.

Before she could turn, he hit her with something, something that
made her head bleed. When she woke, she was chained to the wall.
Isabel cried from the port-a-crib.

Her phone was gone. Nearby were some bottles of water, granola
bars, formula, two bottles, diapers, and wipes.

After a struggle with the chain and stretching, ignoring the
blood dripping from her ankle, she managed to grasp the edge of the
portable crib and bring it closer. Now, she and the baby sat in the
darkness. Waiting.

Waiting for him to return.

———

Gasping as she woke, her body drenched in sweat as her heart tried to pound out of her ribs, was not one of Cici's favorite past times. It was, however, the fastest route she knew to insomnia. She knew this because she'd had this same dream three nights in a row.

With a trembling hand—residual adrenaline—Cici pressed her palm flat to her stomach, willing her diaphragm to unclench, to allow her lungs to inflate fully. Anger built, frustration at her sister's death, sure, but also at Anna Carmen's decision to flit in and out of Cici's life, unable or unwilling to help Cici solve some of the big questions she wanted answered. Just to facilitate these nightmares Cici didn't understand—and didn't want.

"Weeks go by with nothing from you, and *this* is what you send me?" Cici panted, still trying to slow her heart rate, to focus her mind. But all the emotions jumbled together, unable to coalesce around any one of the sensations Cici lived in the dream.

The depictions from those somnolent moments tricked her mind: she'd touched, smelled, felt. It was as if *she* were the person living through the events. Her body still hummed from her experience.

Since her death a year before, Anna Carmen seemed to try to impart knowledge to Cici that would help her—before this set of dreams, all the information had focused on helping Cici find Anna Carmen's killer.

This vision, though, had nothing to do with her dead identical twin or Anna Carmen's death. Nor did it have anything to do with any case Cici had read about in the papers. Which meant…What?

A shiver of unease slid over Cici's sweat-cooled skin.

Bad. The dream portended something terrible to come, meaning Cici could no longer put off getting in touch with her friend and Santa Fe police detective Samuel Chastain.

"I don't remember you being so selfish when you were alive," Cici grumbled at the cool, silent room. "That's what this is— selfish. You want attention? I'd love to lavish you with attention, Aci. I tried." That damn lump lodged itself in Cici's throat. "I wanted to but you shut me out." Cici slammed her eyes shut and pressed her forehead to her knees, compressing her lips together tightly so the next words wouldn't leak out: *Why can't you leave me alone?*

Cici didn't mean that. She loved her sister—wanted her alive, next to Cici more than her next breath. Yet, that wasn't to be.

As a reverend, Cici understood that this desire to lash out at her sister was a form of grief—an unhealthy one she needed to contain.

And…who knew if her sister's spirit lingered? Cici still had no idea how this whole communicate-with-the-dead thing worked. Not well, anyway.

"I miss you," she whispered into the room. She opened her eyes, blinking because the sun now crested over the eastern horizon, and streaks of golden and pink light flashed into the indigo sky. Mona, one of her Great Pyrenees pups, laid her white muzzle, punctuated with a delicate black nose, on the rumpled bedclothes, her dark eyes full of a patience only dogs seemed to expend.

Cici pet Mona's silky ears before she climbed out of bed and stared out her window. There, she pictured her identical twin as she'd last seen her: long, dark hair brushed back from the pale brow, hazel eyes closed as if in sleep, and her black lashes brushing high cheeks. Her nose straight if a tad long, jaw delicate. She'd worn a pretty pink Chanel suit—Cici hadn't known she'd own such an outfit.

Not her favorite memory of her sister, but it was the one she revisited most often.

Cici missed Anna Carmen, always would. Acceptance of the hole in her life—in her heart—proved harder yet to manage.

A ride on her Harley might shake the melancholy and wake her up, get her going.

Cici showered and dressed after letting her dogs outside. Once she'd fed them both and ensured they had plenty of water, Cici slipped on her gloves and jacket between sips of coffee, then grabbed her helmet. She hesitated next to the bike, its body still scratched from last month's frantic trip through barbed wire.

She slid on the helmet, tucking her long hair back before straddling the seat. She revved the engine. Cici's smile grew and her body relaxed as she took to the lightly trafficked streets. Her sister had been right about the relaxation of riding the motorcycle.

Cici needed to do this more often.

Her phone vibrated in her pocket. She pulled it out after reluctantly killing the engine and tugging off her helmet.

"Hello?"

"Reverend Gurule? This is Jan Knowles."

"Blessings, Jan. What can I do for you?"

"I'm sorry it's so early." A long pause followed by a gurgling sigh. "I wanted to wait. I should have waited. It's just…

well...I...I...I found out last night I have cancer. St-stage f-four."

Cici swallowed against the bitter acid biting up the back of her throat. Much as she loved the work she did, helping the congregants in her United Church of Christ family find faith and meaning in their lives, she detested this human suffering that punctuated the happier, sweeter moments.

"I'm glad you called me, Jan. Are you home?"

"Yes." Jan's voice turned watery.

"You're off of Paseo, right?"

Jan gave Cici her address, and Cici said, "I'll swing by now. Mind putting on a pot of coffee? If it's not too much trouble?" Cici asked.

"It's no trouble." Jan heaved a deep soul-shuddering sigh into the phone, as many previous congregants had before her.

Starting a pot of coffee was something positive Jan could do— the task familiar, comforting, and Cici found it helped people reorient their lives a little.

"Thanks, Reverend."

Cici replaced her helmet and restarted the engine. Time to start her day. She'd call Sam, soon. When she had some time.

———

I need to talk to you about a dream I had. Maybe call me later?

Cici pressed the "Send" icon and continued to frown down at her phone. Much as Cici wanted to brush off the dejection and worry that plagued her throughout the day—especially after comforting Jan and getting her to call her estranged older brother—she couldn't. She took comfort in Sam not calling. Not that he would ask her to an open crime scene, should he be at one. Even Cici knew that's not how police *actually* worked.

Cici wouldn't have had much time to talk anyway—she was without a church secretary until the board found a decent replacement. Unfortunately, no qualified candidate had stepped forward yet, and that left Cici to handle most of the office tasks on top of her regular duties.

Busy didn't *entirely* cover her current schedule. And it wasn't like she'd been making time for Sam lately anyway. Not since he'd blown off her attempts to talk after kissing her silly on the hiking trail.

Sam's reply came through hours later: *I'll come by tonight.*

Cici set her phone down after typing back *Okay*. This appeared to be part of their new strange game of barely acknowledging each other. She scrubbed her palms over her face, unsure what to do—how to be around him right now.

———

Later that afternoon, Cici headed over to the Institute of American Indian Arts located behind a large master-planned community and the community college. She was one of the faith leaders asked to participate in the Missing and Murdered Indigenous Women bead project—a few IAIA artists carved and planned to fire the beads with the images of the woman who were known to be murdered or who had disappeared in both the United States and Canada.

"Nice turnout today," Sylvia said. She was one of the artists who, from the look of her clothes and hands, Cici guessed had spent the last few hours working with the brown clay. Sylvia pulled a faded bandana from the back pocket of her old, stained jeans and rubbed her swollen knuckles and palms with it. Bits of clay remained in the seams of her fingers and around her nail beds.

Cici hoped one day to have as much talent at something—or to at least have as much dedication.

"I appreciate the opportunity to take part in this," Cici said, looking around at the fifty or so locals. She waved at the mayor, who was speaking with her friend and church board member Carina. "I had no idea so many women were missing."

Sylvia nodded, her face grave. "I read over four thousand in Canada. We don't have a firm number here, but it's many. No one cares what happens to native women, Reverend."

"I care," Cici said.

Sylvia studied her. "I guess you do. So do I. One of my nieces disappeared from our front lawn in the seventies. This was up near Yakama, where I'm from originally. Growing up, lots of women disappeared, only to turn up a few days or weeks later, dead. FBI looked into it oh…ten years ago? Said they were homicides or accidental. The community was stoic, but you don't have that big a group die without feeling the impact." Sylvia heaved a sigh, the light in her eyes fading with the memories.

"I'm glad that congresswoman in North Dakota is working to bring up legislation," Sylvia said.

Cici nibbled at the inside of her lip, wishing the initial bill for Missing and Murdered Indigenous Women had moved out of its committee. She chose not to voice her concerns after Sylvia's story. Instead, she thanked the older woman and again offered to help. Sylvia smiled and got back to her project.

Cici spoke with some others at the event, then got on her

motorcycle, ignoring a few startled glances when she straddled the electric-blue, vintage 1965 Electra Glide Harley she'd inherited from her twin. She'd learned to ignore others' ideas about what a reverend should do and instead enjoy the time on the open road.

She maneuvered her way back up through the tourists to her church off Rodeo Road. She tidied her desk and locked up the building as the last stragglers from tonight's community yoga class chattered while making their way out the doors and to their cars. She rode home and parked the bike in the single-stall garage tucked on the back side of her small adobe home.

She opened the door that connected to the kitchen to find both her dogs waiting, tails wagging, for her. While she hugged and pet them, she talked about her day.

"Ready for a walk?" she asked.

Strolling through the streets, Cici passed a few of her neighbors and waved. The heat stuck to her skin, coating her in sweat and an unwelcome, oppressive blanket.

She watched Mona frisk around, her plumed tail wagging. Rodolfo stayed close to her side, his pace sedate, his tongue already lolling. Poor boy. Recovering from near-death took time.

She leaned over and pet his ears.

"I'm so thankful you're still with me," she said. He turned his face up toward hers, brown eyes sharp, tongue sliding to the back of his mouth as his canine grin spread.

She walked toward the park at the end of the street, planning to let Rodolfo sit by the side of the cottonwoods while she and Mona attempted some fetch. Mona refused to drop the ball once she collected it, instead darting to and fro, and having a delightful doggy game of tag.

Not Cici's favorite game but Mona lived for it. They transitioned into the park area and Cici grabbed the ball from her pocket.

She threw it just as a thick wave of dizziness slammed her, causing her to shut her eyes. A strange tugging sensation rippled over her, one she'd felt before. Cici shook her head, trying to force the vision out of her mind.

"No. I don't like that," she murmured. "Don't do that to me, Aci. It's awful."

Her sister didn't listen—not that Cici expected her to.

Cici continued to fight, but Anna Carmen tugged at her consciousness. *Come. See. You don't have much time.*

"Aci?" Cici asked, her heart aching at the sound of her twin's voice, even if it was just in her head—in this nightmare. She succumbed to her sister's voice, desperate for a deeper, a stronger, connection to her twin.

But her sister was gone, and Cici was back in Grace's head, how she knew this, she couldn't say. Just that she knew she *was* Grace Bruin and she was scared.

———

Becky finally appeared. As soon as Cici, no she was Grace….As soon as she, Grace received the text, she forwarded it to Becky. She snuck out of the police building, her heart hurting for Henry, for herself, but she couldn't let her baby suffer.

"There were lights in the cabin. And an old SUV. I think." Becky swallowed, eyes wide in the dark. "I think it's the sheriff."

9

Grace's heart plummeted. "Take Isabel. Get out of here."

"I can't leave you here!"

"You don't have a choice. Please, Becky. Please."

"Where can I take her?" Becky asked. "There was a Taos police car here earlier. What if all the police are involved?"

"They might be." Grace bit her lip, tugging Isabel tighter to her chest. "Go to Santa Fe. To Reverend Gurule. She'll figure it out. What to tell Henry and everything. Yeah. Go to her."

"No, Gracie. I'm not leaving you here." Large tears tumbled down Becky's cheeks. "I'm the one who wanted to look into this. I'm the reason you're here."

"We don't have time to argue," Grace said, her voice urgent. "He'll come back soon. He checks in often."

"Has he…" Becky gulped. "Has he hurt you?"

Grace held out her daughter again. "Save her for me," she said, her throat clogged with emotion.

"I don't have a car seat."

"My car does. It's out there, right? There's a key under the driver's side front tire. In one of those little magnetic boxes. Henry made me get one. He was worried about those stories—you know, babies dying in hot cars."

"Okay." Becky sniffled.

Grace pulled the sleeping baby closer to her and kissed her daughter's soft, sweet face. "I love you," she whispered.

"Grace…"

Grace turned her face away. Tears dripped from her quivering chin. "Go!"

Becky picked up the baby and clattered up the stairs. She turned once and looked back, her eyes wide with fear.

Grace almost called her back as the fear of darkness overwhelmed her.

What would he do to her once he realized the baby was gone? That someone else knew his secret?

Grace opened her mouth, about to plead with Becky to take her, too.

Becky disappeared. The wooden doors slammed.

And the wait for the inevitable pain began.

———

Cici blinked her eyes open and stared into the panting faces of her two dogs, who stood watch on either side of her prone body. She sat up, trying to ignore the nausea swirling through her system.

"That was awful," she muttered. With effort, she pulled herself upright. Dark. When she fell into the vision, it had been early evening, before sunset. Now, white stars pixelated the deep, inky blackness of the sky.

"I need to call Sam," Cici moaned.

She'd left her phone back at her house, ignoring Sam's warnings about keeping her phone on her at all times. But she needed this one hour she took each day for herself. Except… it must have been closer to two. Cici staggered back toward her house, trying desperately not to vomit on the way.

2

Cici

Civilization is a hopeless race to discover remedies for the evils it produces. — Rousseau

Sam knocked on the front door before Cici had time to call him.

She made her unsteady way toward the door, Mona circling her legs and emitting high-pitched whines.

"Hey," Sam said from her porch. He didn't step up yet to hug her as he used to do before the opioid case last month.

Cici missed the easy camaraderie they used to share. And, after the day she'd had, she could really use another person's caring. Before she could stop herself, she hurtled forward, forcing Sam to catch her.

He did, patting her back twice before setting her upright. Cici blinked back tears. All-righty, then. Guess she knew where she stood.

Anna Carmen's voice rang through her head: *Fake it till you make, Cee.* With a mental shrug, Cici decided to take her sister's bad advice. It wasn't as though she had a better idea.

Cici walked back to the door and let Mona out, sure the big white fur ball would only scamper over to Sam and not bolt down the street. Mona proved Cici right, waggling right up to

Sam and licking his hand as she shoved her face against his leg.

Sam reached down to pet the dog as his eyes swept the neighborhood. Well, at least Mona received the attention she deserved.

"I ordered a pizza," he said, following Cici into the house. "Sausage, mushrooms, and green chile on whole wheat. Should arrive in the next twenty minutes."

Cici's favorite combination. She smiled. "Thanks."

She walked to the kitchen and pulled down plates.

"Have you talked to Evan recently?" Sam asked. He hesitated, then leaned against the kitchen doorway.

Cici's burgeoning pleasure at seeing Sam collapsed. He didn't want to be here, with her. And why would he ask her about Aci's fiancé?

"No, not recently. We went to dinner a couple of weeks ago," Cici said with a shrug. "He was nicer than usual, but that's probably because he was such an epic jerk to me that he feels bad."

Sam scooted a bit closer. "You think Evan ever feels bad for the way he acts?"

"No," Cici said, trying to keep a straight face, but the smile burst through. "He can be so pompous." She shook her head. "I don't know what Aci saw in him."

Sam considered her for a moment. "He was good to her, for her."

Cici wrinkled her nose. "To each their own, huh?"

Sam smirked. "You got that right."

Something in his voice, or his stare, caused Cici to feel flushed. "I wasn't sure when you'd be by. I…um…I have more to tell you now."

Sam stepped into the narrow galley space and squinted out Cici's kitchen window. "Can I get a drink? Then you can tell me."

Cici grabbed a pitcher of tea from the fridge and poured them each a glass, handing one to Sam. After a sip, she wrinkled her nose and pulled out the agave syrup, adding a thick dollop to her glass. Sam shook his head before she could offer him any.

"That's nasty," he muttered. "If you must drink it sweetened, why can't you just add sugar?"

She swirled the liquid in her glass. "Because the sugar doesn't dissolve as quickly as this stuff. That means the last few sips are straight-up sweet."

Sam turned his focus back to the window, studying the sky. "Looks like rain."

Cici peered out the window. "Meh. Those are hail clouds."

Sam chuckled, easing some of the tension that had built in Cici's neck. But her head still throbbed.

"You don't know that," Sam said. "Why do you even say that?"

"They're all thick and gray, like snow clouds." This conversation was inane. *Any suggestions, Aci?*

Of course, her sister was no help.

"Or rain," Sam said. "Rain also needs thick, dark clouds."

Cici crossed her arms over her chest. "We'll see."

Thunder boomed—a low, harsh rumble—and Cici sighed. Sam smirked.

"But you're not here to talk about my iced-tea drinking habit or the weather. Let me tell you about my dream. It may be nothing, but…" Cici shivered.

She settled her hip comfortably against the counter. "In my dream, there's a missing woman. She has a baby with her."

Sam stood to his full height, eyes widening. "I've not heard of a case like that."

"Maybe it hasn't happened yet," Cici said. She shook her head. "I don't know. I don't remember the whole thing. Just the part where…" She grasped the glass in her hand more tightly, needing the anchor, the reality, so she didn't slip back into that awful place again.

"She's been hurt by her captor. She has a friend…Becky. Becky shows up. Says something about…" Cici racked her brain. She'd lost it—that detail. It was important, too. "I don't know. But Becky takes the baby."

"And leaves the woman—the mom?"

Cici nodded. "She's chained to the wall or floor. Something."

Sam smacked his hands together. "Hold up. You saw this in your dream last night?"

Cici nodded. "And tonight. While I was walking the dogs."

Sam sucked his lower lip into his mouth, considering her for a long moment, before asking, "Has that ever happened before?"

Cici shook her head. "I didn't like it." She rubbed her hands up and down her arms. "It scared me."

"I can tell." Sam took a step, like he meant to get closer but he stopped. "I haven't been brought in on a murder case since…"

Cici inhaled sharply through her nose. Since Cici had nearly died on top of a mountain.

And Sam had kissed her.

Then ignored her.

Sam cleared his throat. He grabbed a pad from his rear pocket. His pencil was missing from the spiral top, so Cici opened the drawer by her hip and offered him a pen. He nodded his thanks, careful not to touch her fingers.

"You think these dreams or nightmares or whatever you want to call them are from your sister?"

Cici hesitated for a moment. "Yes. She talks to me at the beginning. Not much. Just that I need to see this, understand the situation. That kind of thing."

Sam tapped his pen on the pad, his mouth twisting in a grimace of doubt. Still, he'd been there when her sister appeared in the aspens on the top of that hiking trail. Aci had communicated with him, too, so he wasn't willing to totally discount her recounting as grief or crazed imaginings. Yet.

"Tell me everything you remember," Sam said, turning on his no-nonsense detective mode.

Cici cleared her throat and walked them both through all the details she could. She settled her glass on the counter and gripped the counter behind her, but her mind still tugged at her as if wanting to fall back into that space. She needed to remember something…something about who was there…

"Cici?"

She blinked, dazed. "What?"

He frowned down at her, concern dancing through his gunmetal eyes. "You okay?"

"Um."

She slid to the floor, her mind burning as it echoed with the woman's.

3

Cici

*Every person has a right to risk their own life for
the preservation of it. — Rousseau*

Sam must have collected her off the floor because she lay on the
couch, covered by the soft throw blanket she kept over the back.
She opened her eyes.

"What was that?" Sam asked, his voice catching.

She turned and squinted at him, where he knelt on the floor
next to her.

"I don't know," she murmured.

He stood. "You scared me."

Cici didn't respond; she was focused inward, on the emotions
and images that flickered through her mind like a fast-moving
silent film reel.

"Soon." She leaned forward, grasping Sam's wrist. "She's
running out of time," Cici said.

"Who?" Sam asked.

The urgency built, so she rose, the blanket falling to her feet.
A flash of lightning brightened Sam's face, causing his blue eyes
to go momentarily translucent. Not Sam.

She needed to see the killer. The killer stalking her even now.

17

"I don't...I don't know."

A knock sounded on the door. Cici jerked and a small scream escaped her lips. Mona skittered out of the kitchen, her hackles up, as she came to Cici's side. Both she and Rodolfo barked.

When Sam opened the door, the dog's woofs turned half-hearted, just to let Cici know they cared about her and defending the house. The pizza guy showed up at her place often enough that they all knew each other. Sure enough, he scratched both dogs' ears before handing the pizza to Sam.

Sam scooted around the dogs as he shoved his wallet back in his pocket. He set the box on the table and studied her.

"Can you talk about whatever you saw just now?"

"I didn't see anything. At least nothing new."

She walked to the kitchen and grabbed the dishes. Sam gathered their drinks and napkins and they settled at the table.

Cici stared at her plate, now laden with a delicious slice of cheesy goodness, but she made no move to pick up her slice of pizza. She raised her head, meeting Sam's concerned gaze. "Something bad..." Cici sighed. "Something bad's coming."

The rain began to fall after they finished eating, and it poured out in thick sheets of sleety hail.

"On the plus side, you were right about the hail," Sam said. The small skylight in Cici's kitchen pinged as the frozen pellets slammed against the tempered plastic, filling the small house with a tympani solo.

Now that they'd finished eating, Mona rested her muzzle on Cici's knee. As Cici pet her ears, the dog's brown eyes glowed like fresh toffee in the lamplight.

"You afraid, girl?" Cici murmured as she rubbed her hand over the top of the dog's head.

Sam stood in the large entrance between the small kitchen and dining room, rubbing his hand on a dish towel.

"Mind if I take some of the leftover pizza home?"

Cici shook her head. "Please."

Sam disappeared again and Cici heard him moving around in the kitchen. She stayed in her chair, enjoying the moment with her dog.

"Nothing like a hundred-plus-pound ball of anxiety," Sam observed as he returned to the living room.

"Better for her to live here, where it rarely storms, than in, say, Houston," Cici said, still rubbing her hand in soothing motions over the dog's large head. One thing about petting an animal—the repetitive motion soothed Cici nearly as much, maybe more, than the dog herself.

"Got a point," Sam said. "Not just about the fewer thunderstorms. Your dogs are the most pathetic weenies when it comes to heat."

"They don't like bullets and arrows either. I've had enough death and bullets to last me multiple lifetimes," Cici replied.

"You seem to find the worst dregs of our society—and lead them to either commit another crime or confess to an old one."

Cici shuddered, hating that her mind immediately began replaying the events from last month. "Please don't try to draw any connections that don't exist."

"I'm not drawing conclusions or correlations, Cee." Sam

leaned forward, his eyes focused on her face and his tone sincere. "You don't have to justify anything to me." Sam held up his hands palms out. "I'm just telling you that your op-eds in the paper *could* be misconstrued as inflammatory."

"And people could get their heads out of their rear ends and start treating each other with the kindness Jesus wanted. What happened to 'Love thy neighbor'?"

Sam snorted. He stood up and refilled his glass, then stood once more to put away the pitcher of iced tea, slamming the refrigerator door with a resounding thump. Glass in hand, he slid into the chair across from hers.

"First, I'm proud of you for not saying 'asses' like you wanted. That's growth. Second, you do realize I work for law enforcement, right? I don't see much good in people most days."

"Or weeks," Cici grumbled. She rested her hand on top of Mona's head.

"Too true. My job's about as opposite as loving a neighbor as you could get," Sam said.

"That's because your neighbor is a mean-spirited man who refuses to believe there's good left in the world."

Sam settled against the back of the tall chair with a deep chuckle. He sipped from his glass of tea.

This…this conversation with Sam was cozy. Normal. Cici had missed this.

Mona's ears perked at the next thick blast of wind; the hail had turned to rain and was hitting the windowpanes hard enough to sound like small bombs detonating against the house's glass.

Rodolfo rose from his bed next to the small wooden table, his body still stiff from his recent wound.

"Hey, bud," Sam said, reaching out to pet the larger of the two dogs. But Rodolfo stepped away, an unusual occurrence. He adored Sam and had never before turned down a pat.

Now, though, his back fur ridged and he growled, deep and low—the most fearsome sound he could make.

Mona pulled out from under Cici's hand and walked across the room, her toenails clinking softly against the tile. She sniffed at the door and whined. After another sniff, she pawed at the door and whined again.

Sam stood and rounded the table. His face pulled into a look of concern that had him reaching for the gun still in its holster on the side table next to the couch.

"You hear that?"

"Yeah," Cici said. She clenched her jaw together to keep her teeth from chattering.

Rodolfo growled again. He added a short, rough bark followed immediately by a coughing whine. The poor boy's chest still ached from the arrow wound. Mere inches deeper or to the left, and Rodolfo never would have made it off the hiking trail, let alone to this point. Cici stood and went to the dog, placing her hand on his shoulder, where he liked to be touched. He leaned against her, a new occurrence since his surgery, but he kept producing the low rumbling growl and his muscles quivered under Cici's palms.

"Get behind the dining table," Sam directed, his eyes never leaving the door. "Crouch there. I'm going to open the door. If something happens, run out the back and start screaming."

"Sam—"

Mona pawed the door again as if she were digging. She settled in front, her tail swishing back and forth like a large, white, plumed fan, her nose pressed tight against the wood.

Sam checked his weapon, swiping off the safety.

"I have to see what's out there, Cee. Please get behind the table."

"It sounds like—"

Sam unlocked the deadbolt and flung open the door in one smooth motion, all while holding his gun at gut level.

4

Cici

The truth brings no man a fortune. — *Rousseau*

No person stood in the doorway. Beyond the porch, Cici could make out the deep black night dripping with what had turned into a fine sheen of rain. No one and nothing moved.

Mona snuffled into something—a pink polka dotted blanket?—on the floorboards of the porch.

The something Mona sniffed squawked. Well, it was more of a soft mewling cry.

"A baby. That's what I thought I heard," Cici said as she darted around Rodolfo and her dining table. Before Sam could stop her, Cici dove to her knees in front of her door. The blanket was damp but not sopping wet. Maybe the hail reduced the wetness. Whatever the reason, Cici was thankful the child wasn't soaked through.

"Don't pick it up," Sam barked, still searching the night. He'd produced a short, black flashlight with a high LED beam that cast a blue light out into the thick mist. The man was always prepared. He must keep the flashlight in his pocket.

Rodolfo wandered over, his gait stiff but his tail wagging.

The baby cried again with a hiccup at the end.

"Could be a trick," Sam said.

"Neither dog is worried, Sam," Cici said. "Mona's already been all up in the blankets. Now, are you going to stop snarling at the rain and help me figure out how I got a…"

Cici stood up with the bundle in her arms and unwrapped the pink swaddling blanket to get a better look at the child. Tiny diamond studs glinted from the baby's lobes. She had round, rosy cheeks, dark lashes, and a thick head of dark hair. The top of a pink sleeper with white daisy buttons peeped out from the blanket.

Cici was no baby expert, but this plump cherub was not a newborn. Somewhere around nine or ten months, Cici would bet, based on the infants she'd baptized over the years, which was her only real connection with such small children.

She tried to dispel the growing feeling of unease. Cici cuddled the baby closer, hoping to warm the child. Rain in Santa Fe was always chilly—the temperature dropped a good fifteen, twenty degrees with precipitation. Such a pretty child even with closed eyes framed by those long, dark lashes, her cheeks with a high dimple on the left side, just under her eye…Cici's breath stilled.

Twice in one day she'd felt as if the devil slid its finger down her spine; first this morning after the dream and again now. Cici did not care for the feeling any more than she liked her inability to control the situation.

"Like my vision," Cici murmured. "Same outfit." The chill slid up her spine again. "I guess you must be a girl. What was it your mama called you?"

Sam shut her front door with a frown. "Nothing I can see. No headlights and no one skulking. I need to call this in." He reholstered his gun as he peered over Cici's shoulder at the baby.

The baby opened her eyes, maybe because of Sam's voice so close, and a slight frown tugged at those tiny black brows. Cici stared down into the large, nearly golden eyes for a long beat.

"Oh, no," she whispered.

"What's wrong?" Sam's voice vibrated with tension, causing Rodolfo to whine. Mona shoved her nose against the baby's blanket-clad rump.

"Is she hurt?" Sam asked. He pulled out his phone, entering the passcode no doubt to call 911 or dispatch or some other emergency personnel number only those in the field knew to call.

"No, it's fine," Cici said, her voice trembling, definitely not wanting her supposition to be true. She pushed the blanket back farther, trying to ignore her shaking fingers, needing to confirm…ignoring her pounding heart as her fingers skimmed down the child's cotton-clad arm to the cuffed sleeve. "Everything's fine."

"Do many kids have earrings so young?" Sam asked as he dialed a number.

Cici shrugged, uncaring about the child's jewelry, much more interested in the baby's birthmarks.

Sam glared at the floor near their feet. "This is Detective Sam Chastain. I need to report in a child left on Reverend Cecilia Gurule's doorstep just now. Requesting backup and help to secure the perimeter. Call in an ambulance, too, please." He rattled off Cici's address. "Three minutes," he said before he clicked off.

"Is all that necessary?" Cici asked. She wasn't sure why she asked—it was, she understood that.

His expression remained unhappy. "Yeah. Standard operating procedure."

Sam turned to focus outside, clearly itching to be out there, investigating.

"See this little red spot on her neck?" Cici touched her finger lightly to a spot just below the baby's right ear. No bigger than the head of a pencil eraser, the color was as red as blood.

Sam moved in closer so that his chest pressed against Cici's arm. He stared down at the child.

"That's an identifying mark," Sam muttered.

Cici nodded. "She has another on her elbow." Cici's fingers skimmed over the discoloration she'd recently bared.

"I've never seen those before. What are they?" Sam asked.

"Birthmarks. They're called port-wine stains, but this baby's father called them angel kisses."

"All right." Sam peered into her face, eyes narrowed as he drew connections. "You knew about the birthmark already, which means you know who the child belongs to." Sam's frown deepened at seeing Cici's downturned expression. "But you're not happy you know who this baby belongs to."

Her heart stomped with frenetic precision against her ribs like a Folklorico dancer. "Oh, I know her, yes, because I baptized her a couple of months ago," Cici murmured, aware she was stalling.

She did not want to tell Sam this baby's name.

"Okay…," Sam said, drawing out the word.

Cici wrapped both arms around the child. She raised her gaze to his. He stared back, the confusion in his eyes laced with growing concern. She couldn't wait, no matter how much she wanted to evade the inevitable.

"This is Isabel Ignacia Bruin, and she's the baby that was in my nightmares." As soon as Cici said the words, a soft whine filled her ears. Not from the dogs, no. From the baby. Deciding not to take any chances with her noodly legs, Cici collapsed onto her couch.

"You're absolutely sure?" Sam's voice was raspy. "I mean, *positive*?"

Cici understood his concern—and shared it. When Sam's eyes met hers, they were as wide as her eyes felt, and seemed to mirror her fear right back at her.

With a slow nod, Cici whispered the word that shattered the peace of their night.

"Yes."

5

Cici

Trust your heart rather than your head.
— *Rousseau*

His game-face on, Sam began pressing buttons on his phone.

"What are you doing?" Cici asked.

"Damn, it would be raining. That's going to make finding evidence that much more difficult."

"Evidence?" Cici squeaked.

Sam raised an eyebrow in her general direction as he moved back toward her front window. "Well, this child was left on your porch. I have to know who brought the kid here. Why would be exceedingly useful, too," Sam replied. "Especially since you think she was with her mother earlier. And *doubly* especially since you believe the baby was abducted."

"Where did the kidnapping happen?" she asked, trying to get a handle on her spinning thoughts.

At least baby Isabel looked healthy. Looks could be deceiving, but Cici was encouraged by the child's healthy complexion and ability to sleep even in a strange place with strange smells.

Sam cocked his head to the side, considering, though his eyes remained on little Isabel's tiny, peaceful face.

"You mentioned Taos," Sam said.

"I did," Cici said, settling the child into her lap and trying to calm her shaking hands and legs. "You haven't heard anything about an abduction or a missing woman?"

Sam had already said he hadn't, but Cici asked anyway. Sam shook his head.

"A crime in Taos wouldn't necessarily be broadcast down to the Santa Fe PD."

Well, that made sense. "But now that the baby's here?"

Sam's lips flattened into a concerned line. "Then SFPD just got involved. Neck deep."

If her nightmare was correct, then Grace was chained in some cabin. No, not the cabin. Cici frowned, trying to remember. Near a cabin.

"So…" He glanced up at Cici. "Where do *you* fit into all this, Cici?"

"Don't look at me like that." Cici gulped. "I had *nothing* to do with this."

"I'm not so sure, Rev," Sam said slowly, using the affectionate moniker given to Cici by her teen congregants. "You've dreamt of her. You admitted as much earlier. And, here she is. She just shows up here within hours. That seems pretty much like a miracle."

6

Sam

It is in order not to become victim of an assassin
that we consent to die if we become assassins.
— Rousseau

"I do not create miracles," Cici said, her voice as stiff as her body. "That's ludicrous. And untrue."

Sam rubbed his lower lip before sliding his fingers through his newly shorn hair. It was short—shorter than he'd worn it even in middle and high school. The conservative style played well with his boss and the politicians he met occasionally, but Sam missed the ponytail—and the small amount of rebellion toward his father and his button-down life that the longer hair connoted.

"Don't get mad at me." Sam stuck out his fingers. He liked to plan; doing so helped to calm him down. He ticked off his ring finger. "First, we have the child looked over, and, second, I put in a call to the Child Youth and Family Department," Sam said, bending his middle finger toward his palm.

"I mean, I don't know the story behind the supposed abduction, so I don't know if I'm supposed to give the child back to her mom or CYFD until we can figure out what is going on here. Third, I'll contact the detective at TPD who worked the case."

"You can't send the child back to her mother," Cici murmured.

"Why's that?" Sam asked, the first inkling of annoyance creeping in.

"Her mother's missing."

Sam shook his head. "She hasn't been called in as missing."

Cici frowned. "You're sure? You said it yourself, if the crime happened in Taos."

"Fine. I haven't been briefed on a disappearance of a grown woman here in Santa Fe."

And he didn't want Cici to be correct about the mother's disappearance because one thing Sam *was* sure of: if this child's mother turned out to be missing the baby could not go back to her father. More than likely, this was a domestic violence case.

So he'd have to ask Child Services to try to find suitable next of kin. But already Sam had a creeping suspicion this case would prove more complicated than the average kidnapping. With Cici involved, there'd be nothing cut-and-dried or easy about this situation.

Sam prided himself in his ability to use logic, thought and care for others. That whole *Do unto others* spiel that reverends like Cici gave to young children—and many older congregants alike—on any given Sunday didn't apply in his work, which was why anything Sam conjured in his imagination right now about the baby's parents would be negative and more chilling than Cici would ever want to think of.

As Cici shifted again, the baby's blanket fell to the ground—along with a sealed white envelope.

Mona trotted over and sniffed the pink-and-white cotton. Sam shoved the dog's tail out of the way as he stooped down and picked up the blanket and the piece of paper that had fluttered from the material.

Mona shoved her nose toward the baby, but Cici managed to deflect the dog's interest for the most part.

Sam's heart rate sped back up. All this damn adrenaline—it couldn't be good for him.

"Go to place, Mona," Cici said, her voice carrying the don't-push-me tone she rarely used. Finding the baby rattled Cici more than she'd like to admit, Sam could tell. Well, he understood her concern.

The dog raised an eyebrow as if to say, *really*? When Cici pointed, Mona huffed before returning to the dining room. Just to be obnoxious, she shoved her way into Rodolfo's bed. The other dog must have been exhausted from his recent exertions because he didn't snarl at his sister. Nor did he even open an eye. Mona lay her head on Rodolfo's back and eyed Cici, then Sam, with a plaintive gaze.

Nothing overtly sinister in the envelope. Yet.

No raindrops stained the paper, which appeared dry and intact.

"Tweezers?" Sam asked.

"In my bathroom. Should be in the top drawer."

Sam nodded. He strode down the hall, returning a moment later with the tweezers to grab the side of the note. He used a tissue in his other hand and opened it with great care, trying not to tweak or wrinkle the paper. Cici leaned over his shoulder.

The handwriting was bubbly, done in blue ink. Based on what Sam knew of handwriting, his first guess was this appeared young and feminine, almost that of a child.

But the words, themselves, spoke of something much more ominous, giving heed to Sam's ideas of the Bruins as a criminal couple. Something, he had no doubt, Cici would reject vociferously.

Isabel's not safe. We made a mistake researching those deaths. He must work for the police.

7

Cici

---

*All of my misfortunes come from having thought
too well of my fellows — Rousseau*

"Police?" Cici asked in a voice that rose in question—and fear. Her breath ripped out of her lungs.

Isabel stirred, grunting as she brought her knees up to her chest. Cici patted the child's delicate back and Isabel parted her little lips just enough for the gurgle to slip through.

"Shit," Sam mumbled.

Sam's gaze darted from the note to Isabel and back to the note. "Let me get a baggie. I want this sealed before we mess up our chances to pull a print off it."

He disappeared into the kitchen only to return moments late, bypassing Cici to glance out the window.

"My team's outside," Sam said, nodding to the growing red and blue flashing lights converging outside her house.

Cici glanced up to focus on Sam's comment. "Sam, in my vision, the one I had today at the park…"

"Yeah?"

"Becky said something about the police. About the police being involved somehow."

"Involved in what?"

Cici smoothed her hand over the baby's crown, enjoying the warm silkiness of her head.

"I think the police, someone there…" She frowned. "A car. A patrol car," Cici said slowly. "And…" She struggled, grasping at the faint tendrils of memory that tried to evade capture. "The sheriff."

"Which is it?" Sam asked.

"Both. They're involved. The sheriff wasn't mentioned, but Grace…she thought of the sheriff." Cici's voice trailed off. Maybe she'd made that part up. But she felt sure there was something to do with the sheriff, too. "I-I don't know more." She raised her gaze to meet his troubled one.

Sam blew out a long breath. "You okay for the moment?"

He waited for Cici's nod. "I'm going outside to talk to the crew and we'll walk the perimeter." He scowled and shook his head. "Not that we're likely to find much in this weather. Rains all of ten times per year and this happened tonight," he muttered, then he closed the door behind him with a businesslike click.

A moment later, he opened the door, phone to his ear, as he poked his head inside.

"The ambulance is on the way to transport the baby to the hospital. I need to call the parents. Henry and Grace Bruin. Are those the right people?"

Cici snuggled the child tighter in her arms. "Yes. If you need it, I have their contact information on my computer."

"Nope, all good. Let's hope the mom's fine."

He closed the door again, and the room returned to cozy

silence. Except Cici didn't feel cozy. She stared at the baby, wondering who could have dropped her off...and worse, why.

"Let's hope," Cici murmured. She didn't hold out much optimism.

Sirens screamed into the night, fighting with the distant rumbles of thunder for the supremacy of sound. Cici spoke in a quiet, firm voice to Mona and Rodolfo, calming the dogs even as she rocked and shushed the now-crying child.

The dream she'd had last night began to shape itself in her mind again as if Anna Carmen was reinforcing certain details. The woman's fear of whoever hit her and her greater fear for her child.

All those emotions, snippets of the room, and Grace's desperation to get Isabel from the dark, damp space added to Cici's concern she was holding the baby of a dead woman.

8

Cici

*The good man can be proud of his virtue because it
is his. But of what is the intelligent man proud?*
— *Rousseau*

The ambulance pulled into the driveway, lights flashing and
sirens blaring. Isabel began to sob even harder. Mona matched
pitch with the infant's wails, creating a cacophony of distress that
caused a shredding-type of pain to spring up behind Cici's eyes.

Finally, the sirens turned off. Cici continued to rock the baby
back and forth in her arms. Mona nudged Cici's leg in increasing
agitation when Cici did not comply immediately with her usual
pats. Sam led two paramedics into Cici's small living room,
their faces damp with rain and their feet leaving tracks on her
floor. Sam's face held a grimace of frustration. Cici bet that had
something to do with the sirens and any hope for finding the
person who dropped off the child.

While the men came straight to the baby, Sam beelined to
Mona, who wagged and jumped up in a show of poor behavior
and extreme need for a human to soothe her.

Isabel cried harder as the men took her from Cici's arms.
Much as Cici wanted to put her hands over her ears, she instead

dropped her hand to Mona's head, also caressing her dog who nuzzled in closer.

"I need to get back outside," Sam said, wiping rainwater from his face.

"Of course," Cici said.

Rodolfo wandered over. He sniffed the paramedics as they check the baby, found them as uninteresting as most of Cici's guests, and returned to his bed, lowering himself to the pillow with a muffled groan.

Cici, however, became more agitated the longer the baby cried. Isabel's small head turned bright red and her tiny fists and feet flailed in obvious distress.

"Okay, she's stable," Jim, the older of the two EMTs, said. "You want to meet us at the hospital?"

Cici lurched forward, touching Isabel's stomach.

"May I ride with her?" she asked, concerned by the child's shrieking.

The paramedics exchanged a long look. "You're not next of kin," Jim said, voice filled with regret.

Cici let her shoulders fall. Part of her was relieved to get away from the crying. "Sure. I'll meet you there after I put my dogs out again. Christus?"

"Yep," Jim replied. "See you in a bit."

The EMTs rolled out the long stretcher, hunched protectively over their tiny charge. Cici turned into her bedroom and began to gather up a few belongings she might need for an extended stay in the emergency department or wherever she ended up keeping vigil.

After leaving Sam a message, Cici trudged toward her Subaru, shoulders hunched against the intermittent drops, the last remnants of the storm.

Tonight was going to be long.

———

Unhappy babies exhausted their caretakers before themselves— at least in Cici's limited experience. The last time she felt this soul-deep lack of will to continue was the day Anna Carmen died.

Isabel sniveled in her sleep, a soft hiccupping sob slipping out of her tiny mouth. Cici's ears still rang with the sound of Isabel's cries, which carried on for hours, during which time, a team of doctors and nurses checked the baby. So far, Cici had been assured the child appeared healthy.

Sam showed up, looking as exhausted as Cici felt, his shirt water-stained and his hair flattened to his head, with two large to-go cups emblazoned with the logo of a local coffee shop.

"That smells divine," Cici moaned, practically falling on Sam as she reached for one of the cups.

"No. Take this one. It's a mocha. Figured you deserved it."

Cici snatched the cup, her mouth already beginning to water. "Thanks."

"I called over here and the nurse told me Isabel was still wailing. Jeez. I don't know how you handled that." His eyes held shocked admiration—emotions Cici was sure she didn't deserve.

To cover her growing embarrassment, she asked, "How'd you get this at…" She glanced up at the clock. "Huh. Is it just now nearing midnight? Seems later."

Cici sipped, thrilled at the cool froth of whipped cream before the hot spike of caffeine and chocolate hit her taste buds.

"Oh, I needed that," she said on a delighted sigh.

"Figured," Sam said with a smirk.

"Thanks," Cici said. "You find anything outside?"

"Maybe," Sam said.

He didn't often talk details about ongoing investigations—not that Cici blamed him. She couldn't discuss her current congregant issues, nor would she ever do anything to break trust or invade the privacy of her few-hundred-person-strong UCC faith members.

"The rain made processing the scene more difficult, but we may have gotten a couple of IDs on the car. People look out for you."

"You expected that about the rain." Cici relaxed into his side, thankful for his presence. And the hot coffee. "I'm glad I live in a community that cares."

"Me, too. Isabel's parents haven't shown up yet?" Sam asked, frowning. "I called them before I left your place. I had to leave a message on both their phones."

Cici sipped again, also frowning. "It must have been nearly ten by the time you called them—at least I'm guessing if you were outside for a while first. Maybe they have that Do Not Disturb thing on their phones."

Sam shrugged. "Makes sense, I guess. Are you planning to stick around until the Bruins show up?"

"For now. You?"

"I'm sticking," Sam said. He paused for a minute, then said, "I asked to be put on this case."

They drank their coffee in the relative silence of a late night in the hospital.

"I think you need to consider the fact Grace may not call back," Cici said into the quiet.

Sam made a noncommittal sound. When Cici elbowed him in the ribs, he grunted. "Man, you can be a pain in the as—er, rump."

Cici shook her head and rolled her eyes. Sam had been trying not to curse as much around her in an effort to get her not to curse either. As she'd told him many times, she liked a few choice words and too damn bad if others agreed or not. Sam smirked at her annoyance.

"I heard you about the dreams. I get what you're saying, but…" Sam trailed off, then shrugged. "There's just something about this situation that I don't like."

———

The freckles along her cheeks and neck created an incongruous comparison, but…the long dark hair, the winged black brows, and the swollen flesh that drowned out the woman's proud cheekbones remind Cici of her twin, Anna Carmen.

With a sharp bite of recognition, Cici realized that meant the woman looked like her.

Before she processed the revelation, an article fell from the battered woman's front pocket. With shaking hands, Cici plucked the small plastic ring from the blood-soaked denim, shuddering.

A pacifier.

———

Cici woke with the image of removing the baby's Nuk from the pockmarked, reeking asphalt. She rubbed her hands over her face, freaked by the connection to Isabel, to her earlier dreams, even more than the similarities in her and the woman's features.

A man's deep, angry voice rose, edged closer to the door, drawing Cici back to the present moment. She stood as the voice roared again, and she managed to dump the dregs of her coffee over in her haste to rise. A small puddle of dark, rich brown formed on the floor in front of the loveseat.

"I want to see my baby," the man cried.

"Sir! I need to see some ID."

"That's Henry," Cici said.

"You sure?" Sam asked. He stood and stretched, scowling at the door.

Cici rubbed her eyes. "Pretty sure. But I've never heard him so worked up before."

The purple metal door to the private pediatric room shuddered against the thin film of gypsum wallboard as it was yanked hard against the door's casing. A loud bang caused Cici to start and the baby's eyes to pop open. She squinted around the crib in the dim light, her small chin quivering, her rosebud mouth already parting with the first wail.

Cici braced herself for the noise.

After he rose, Sam's hand moved to his gun—one he could bring in to a weapon-free zone because of his badge. Cici shuddered a little as Sam removed the weapon from its holster in one quick movement.

After the experiences of last month, she would never be

comfortable around guns.

Sam kept his pistol pointed toward the floor, finger on the safety, as Henry Bruin grasped the door in his huge hand and shoved his way into the small hospital room.

Sam wasn't a small man—he was well-muscled from consistent weight workouts—but Henry Bruin's bulk dwarfed Sam's tall, lean frame. Probably two-fifty with a thick waist, Henry might be able to bench press Sam.

The baby's keening sobs filled the air. Cici's head began to pound.

"I want my Isabel," Henry growled, eyes and hair wild.

Cici clutched the edge of the baby's plastic crib, a protective gesture she managed unconsciously. Isabel stopped midscream and stretched her small body and raising her head.

"Dada? Dada!" Isabel yelled the last word and lunged toward her father. Henry plucked Isabel from the crib and held her with gentle care. This time, Henry's chin quivered as he snuggled the baby tight to his chest.

"Ah, Izzy." The big man gulped. Tears poured down his face as he brought his forehead down to touch his daughter's. The baby slapped her tiny palms to the sides of his face while a deep, infectious belly laugh burst out of her mouth.

"Dada, Dada!" she cried over and over, bouncing in her excitement.

Sam walked into the small, private bathroom and grabbed a bunch of paper towels. After wiping up the spilled coffee, he motioned Cici back over to the small loveseat. They plopped down on the hard nylon surface as they watched the man press

ALEXA PADGETT

kisses to Isabel's face and talk sweet nonsense in her ear.

Finally, as if recovering himself, Henry turned toward Cici and Sam. His eyes widened to see Cici there and he dipped his head in acknowledgment, probably respect. Cici always found Henry to be deferential to her position. She returned the gesture.

Henry cleared his throat, eyes darting around the room. "So where's Grace?"

"Grace?" Cici asked, her mind still sluggish. Then, it all came back to her.

Her nightmare.

The Nuk.

Her stomach heaved. She'd seen a dead woman.

Henry hugged the baby tighter to his chest as he glared over her small head at Sam.

"I'm going to have to kill that woman if she had anything to do with taking my baby from me."

9

Cici

*I cannot repeat too often that to control the child
one must often control oneself. — Rousseau*

Grace? Took the child. *Whoa.*

Cici met Sam's puzzled gaze around Henry's large body. She needed to tell him her most recent nightmare.

She prayed she'd missed the mark on this one and Grace was somewhere sipping mimosas. She did not feel good about her chances of getting that prayer answered.

"Mr. Bruin, I'm Detective Sam Chastain," Sam said, clearly trying to defuse the escalating tension building in the room.

Henry turned toward him. "Yeah, I know you. You've been at the church and the rev here's mentioned you."

Sam stood from his place and waved his hand for Henry to sit on the small loveseat. The bigger man was so enthralled with his daughter that he quickly settled onto the couch. Cici chose to perch on the other end.

"I'd like to ask you some questions, if I may," Sam said.

"I have a few myself," Henry said. He smiled down at Isabel who kicked her feet and gurgled and kept up a persistent string of dada dada dada.

"Where'd you find Izzy?" Henry asked.

"Well," Cici said, twisting her hands in her lap. "Your daughter was left on my porch."

"In that rainstorm tonight?" Henry touched Izzy's forehead, then her cheek with the back of his hand. "She doesn't seem sick. Who left her? Why did they bring her here? Goddamn Grace for not answering my calls!"

Cici flinched when Isabel started to cry, pulling her knees up to her stomach.

"She's hungry. And sopping wet," Henry said. "She needs a fresh diaper."

"We'll have to get you some diapers from the nurse," Sam said.

"Oh, I have a bag. Keep it in my car. Let me grab it," Henry said, repositioning the baby so he could pull out his car keys.

Sam walked with him toward the door. "I'll come with you."

Henry turned to glare down at Sam. "You think I'd bolt with my kid?"

Sam kept his gaze level, his tone neutral. "After everything I've seen in domestic disputes? I can't say what you'd try. Or not. More importantly, you cannot remove the child from this facility until the doctor clears her for release, which he hasn't done yet."

Something Cici now suspected had more to do with Sam than Isabel needing to stay in the hospital. Her stomach hitched and she frowned at Sam's back.

"Yeah," Henry said, blowing out a breath. "Yeah, okay. Can you get some formula and a bottle of water, too?"

Sam nodded, his expression blank. He returned a few minutes later with the items, and Henry changed Isabel's pants. From what Cici could tell, he appeared quite proficient at the task. After wiping his hands with a baby wipe, Henry scooped from the round tin of organic baby formula and poured the powder into the bottle.

"I won't make her a bottle with tap water. There's all kinds of stuff in that. Metals and bacteria." Henry curled his lip. "How can we expect our kids to be healthy when we let them drink toxins?"

Cici hoped that was a rhetorical question because she had no answers.

After shaking the substance to an even, white consistency, he stuck the bottle in Isabel's mouth. She grabbed the sides, grunted, and began to suck in earnest. Henry's arm around Isabel's back held the bottle with ease while his other one touched the crown of her head.

"Seriously," he said, his voice dazed. "I can't believe I'm holding her again."

He leaned down to kiss the top of her head. Her eyes followed his every movement while she drank from her bottle.

"This is a dream," he muttered. "The best kind."

"What happened, then, Henry?" Cici asked, her voice as soothing as she could make it. "The day she disappeared?"

Henry' breath hitched. "I was down near Carlsbad, doing some work on the water rights."

Sam pulled out his notebook from his jacket pocket. That meant he planned to double-check everything Henry said. Had he not heard Cici's accounting of the situation?

"Go on," Sam said. "You were in Carlsbad the day Isabel disappeared?"

Henry swallowed, a thick sound, and tears pooled in his eyes.

"Yeah." He cleared his throat. "Grace called me around three in the afternoon. She said…" His voice cracked. "She said Izzy was…gone."

"Do you know who was with Grace that day?"

Henry frowned. "I never thought to ask. I assumed Grace was alone, just out getting some stuff for Izzy."

"She didn't have friends or family in the area?" Sam asked.

"She's from Taos."

Again, Cici met Sam's eyes. The police mentioned in the note must be the Taos police. Cici frowned. The Pueblo there, like all Pueblos, had its own government, which meant a second police force. And, in her dream, she'd thought the sheriff was a potential problem.

The complications kept piling.

Henry continued, "That's where most of her family is. We haven't seen much of her mother, and the only other person Grace hangs out with in Santa Fe is Becky. She has some other friends up in Taos." He pursed his lips.

Cici tried not to gasp at the name. Becky. She'd heard that one, too. She'd been the woman to come and get Isabel, take her from the cabin.

"Winnie…something," Henry said. "Can't remember her last name, but she and Grace used to be close. Real close all through school."

Sam finished writing down the two names, ones Cici knew he'd look into as soon as possible. Sam leaned in. "Why don't you see Grace's mother?"

Henry's scowl darkened. "Grace was getting all kinds of crap from her mom. 'I can't believe you baptized the baby. How's she going to learn the ancient ways? You need to get out of the city and bring that child to me.' That kind of stuff."

"Did it happen often?" Sam asked.

Henry nodded. "From the moment I proposed. Gracie's mother has never been my biggest fan."

Isabel let go of the bottle's nipple with a pop.

"Dada," she said. She smiled and rooted around for the tip again, sucking it greedily into her mouth as she kept her gaze firmly on Henry's face.

"This girl seems head over heels for you," Cici said. She blinked and yawned with bleary weariness. Outside, the night was still too deep a violet-black for morning. It must have been around four. Cici feared how much more tired she'd be if she looked at a clock.

"She's got me wrapped around her tiny finger, that's true. I took one look at those big eyes and I was a goner. Total love at first sight."

Cici smiled at him but then hid the same sadness that had welled in her chest just hours ago when she held the baby by sipping from the water Sam had brought her a few minutes before.

"What made you think Grace is avoiding your calls?" Sam asked.

"I haven't seen her, not since Grace told me she was up in Taos when Isabel disappeared."

Cici caught her breath. She knew this from her dream but wanted further confirmation. "I thought the baby disappeared here, in Santa Fe."

"No. Gracie'd gone up to visit her friend. Winnie. She's been doing that about once a week or so."

Sam kept his face neutral but Cici could read his body language and knew he was forming the same thoughts she was: Grace must have been having an affair up there and using her friend as an excuse.

"So, Grace was in the Pueblo when Isabel disappeared?" she asked.

What had the note said? *Isabel's not safe. We made a mistake researching the deaths. He must work for the police.*

"No, not then," Henry said. "At the Walmart in town. But that's where I met Grace. Her family's connection to the Tiwa goes back almost six hundred years." Henry said these words with pride.

"Grace didn't come home with you after the initial investigation?" Sam asked.

Henry cleared his throat, no doubt trying to rid some of the emotion building within his chest. "I had to go to work, and Gracie…she refused to come home."

"Do you know why?" Sam asked.

"No. Well, maybe a guess," Henry said with a slight shrug.

"Will you tell me?" Sam asked.

"Grace got a message while we were at the police headquarters. We were waiting for the FBI guy to turn up. She got a text message and up and walked out of the room."

"That was the last time you saw her?" Sam asked.

Henry leveled Sam with a look. "Yes."

"She hasn't returned another one of your messages?" Sam asked.

Henry remained stoic but Cici saw the hurt in his eyes. "No. Not one thing," Henry said, his voice flat. "It's been almost four days."

10

Sam

Doubt with regard to what we ought to know is a condition too violent for the human mind; it cannot long be endured; in spite of itself the mind decides one way or another, and it prefers to be deceived rather than to believe nothing.

— *Rousseau*

"Is that strange?" Sam asked. "From what you've said, you and Grace were close."

"Yeah." Henry blew out a breath. "We were. I thought we discussed everything."

"Has Grace ever done something like this before?"

"No, never. Everything about this whole situation is crazy," Henry said. "I thought we were real happy, then Grace said Izzy…"

Henry huffed a shuddering breath.

"Grace refusing my calls, choosing to stay with her mom— that's really strange, Detective. Whole time I was with Gracie, we barely saw her family."

"Why do you think she's with her mother?" Sam asked.

Isabel finished her bottle. She spat out the nipple and grinned up at her dad, clapping her hands. Two small white teeth poked through her bottom gum, one shorter one barely grazed the top.

Sam made some more notes in his notebook, not liking the network of connections beginning to form. Taos. Tribal police. Grace's talk with her mother. Grace missing. Cici's dream.

"Where else could she be?" Henry asked.

Dead, Sam thought. Or close to it. But he didn't say it.

Not yet. Not just because Cici worried on the point after her visions. But because he had nothing concrete as evidence to prove Grace wasn't alive and well at her mother's house.

He needed to get up to Taos, pronto.

"Sam, I need to talk to you," Cici mumbled.

He didn't think Cici understood how her face softened, her eyes glistening with tears when she looked at Henry. Cici didn't seem to understand how much attention Sam paid to her—which was probably for the best, really.

He followed her into the hall. She turned and faced him, her mouth set in a rigid line he didn't like.

"I had another dream. It was bad. A woman was dead. She had a pacifier in her pocket."

Sam sighed. Cici's dreams were troubling. The content and how closely it followed this case disturbed him but so, too, did the increased frequency. Not that either helped him, really.

"All right. Walk me through. Where were you?"

"The Five and Dime," she said immediately.

Well, that was specific. Except they hadn't had any activity reported there.

"What did she look like? The dead woman?"

Cici shot him a look that said she knew he was placating her.

Of course he was. He worked in facts. He had to because he couldn't convict people on dreams.

"Like me."

Sam's body chilled and the hairs rose on his arms and the nape of his neck. "You saw yourself dead?" he asked.

"No, I saw a woman who looked like me, dead in the alley by the Five and Dime. She'd bled out." Cici pressed her lips together. "I don't know how, but she'd been beaten. Badly."

Sam processed that information while Cici steadied her breathing.

"I'm going to the bathroom," Cici muttered.

Sam headed back into the room to find Henry smiling down at his daughter.

"Another tooth!" Henry said, delight marking each of his words. "Look at you, growing up so fast, precious girl."

The baby cooed and kicked her legs. Henry lifted her to his shoulder where the baby snuggled her cheek. He patted her back with soft, soothing strokes. She belched loud and then again, quieter.

The tension built thicker as the two men eyed each other with a heavy wariness. Henry stood and moved to the rocking chair—the only other seating option in the room. Sam settled onto the far end of the love seat, a generous name for the uncomfortable piece of furniture, leaving space for Cici nearest the door.

"Grace, Isabel's mom," Sam said, gesturing with his chin toward the baby. "You said you met her when you were doing work in Taos Pueblo."

"Yeah. We met up there when I was doing survey work for the

state so we could look at our grazing land rights leases. All about the water. As it always is in the West."

"And you helped write the proposal for increasing the fees," Sam said with a snap of his fingers. "Yeah. I read about that. You moved here from…" Sam paused.

"Montana," Henry replied.

"And was this the type of work you did up there?" Sam asked.

"Sure. But we didn't have to deal with the tribes up there," Henry said. "Not like here."

"Have they given you trouble?" Sam asked. He needed a better sense of Henry's relationship with the communities he worked in. As a police officer, Sam understood the potential mistrust from certain groups—especially those who were frightened that he planned to use the city's power to remove their hard-built community. From what he'd read and seen over the years, some of that mistrust seeped into the government workers' relationships—especially when it came to natural resources and historic cultural ceremonies and customs.

"They don't always like us coming in, asking questions," Henry said, leaning back in the chair.

He crossed one long, thick leg over the other, knee-to-ankle, to get more comfortable. Sam could have told him it was a wasted effort.

"I mean, I get where they're coming from," Henry muttered. "Doesn't make my job easier though."

"So you worked for the Bureau of Land Management, and met Grace up there in Taos."

Cici returned. She sat and crossed her legs. Her hair was a

long tangle and her eyes were droopy, but she appeared alert—better than Sam felt at any rate.

Henry shook his head. "Originally. But we didn't talk much. There was a definite attraction, sure, but nothing came of it. Then, about…I guess it was six or eight months later, I met Grace at the saloon downtown here in Santa Fe. She'd just started as one of the waitresses. She told me she and her mom had a falling out."

"Do you know what that was about?" Sam asked.

"The disagreement?" Henry frowned. "Grace didn't say much. Just that her mom didn't want her looking too deeply into the family's history. Nor did her mom think it was safe for Grace to move to the big, bad city. Grace's grandma was killed back in the…" Henry frowned, thinking. "I guess it must've been the eighties sometime."

Sam made a note of that detail.

"But Grace moved to Santa Fe anyway? Despite her mother's objections?"

"She planned to get certified in solar installations." He said this with pride.

"So, you dated a bit and got engaged?" Sam asked.

Henry's cheeks reddened and his eyes darted to Cici, which caused his face to darken another couple of shades. "Sort of. We kinda…we got together. You know, because we'd already hung out up in Taos a couple of times."

From the corner of his eye, Sam saw Cici bite her lip to keep from smirking. Sam's amusement grew, too, because he knew Cici's congregants always grew uncomfortable about discussing their sex lives with her. She'd told Sam once that their lack of candor was part of why she wanted to work with the older teens and college students to discuss how often the Bible talked about sexuality and its importance as a person and in a relationship.

"All right," Sam said, trying to keep any hint of amusement from his voice. Guessing from Cici's sharp elbow to his hip, he failed. "You started a sexual relationship, and I'm guessing Grace got pregnant?"

"Pretty quick," Henry said, darting a look back at Cici. His face was brighter than a ripe red chile. "So, I, ah, I said we needed to get married. Grace agreed. She seemed relieved."

Isabel pushed forward so that she sat up in Henry's lap. She kept one hand on his leg but used the other to reach toward the crib. She nearly lost her balance, so he set her on the floor. She turned back to her dad, placing both hands on his pants and bouncing up and down, making an "ah ah ah" noise on repeat.

"And did you have the wedding back at the Pueblo?"

"No," Cici said. "I officiated." She smiled at Henry. "It was one of the first ceremonies I performed here in Santa Fe."

"We had a real nice wedding, Reverend."

"Glad you liked it," Cici said, her voice warm.

Sam could tell Cici enjoyed it, too. Well, that's what he'd thought until she frowned, her eyes darkening with concern and maybe even a hint of disapproval.

"I'm concerned, though, about these recent troubles between you and Grace. You know my door's always open should you want to talk about…anything."

Isabel reached toward the crib's railing again. She missed and this time toppled forward. Henry leaned forward and grabbed her around the middle, his grasp easy as if this was a normal occurrence.

Man, babies were not for sissies and required constant, focused attention. Sam's heart raced at the potential for pain Henry managed to avert.

Henry settled Isabel back on her feet and the baby went back to bouncing.

"It's Grace's family," Henry said, his scowl deepening. "When it was us two, then even with Izzy here, everything was great. We were happy. But, like I said before, Grace's mom hates me."

"Any idea why?" Sam asked.

Henry shook his head. "Nothing I did intentionally, at least. I mean, the people we met up with at the Pueblo weren't too happy with how we wanted to handle the water rights. The elders were up in arms over the changes."

Henry ran his thumb over the baby's head where she rested it against his leg.

"Could be how fast we got married. The fact that we had a baby just six months later." He shook his head. "Well, no, that's not true. More of the issue was simply that I'm Izzy's father."

He scooped Isabel back into his lap, but the baby struggled for a moment, kicking her legs in an effort to get down. Henry changed his grip, picking up the baby and laying her against his shoulder. He patted her back with a gentle hand. "You're going to be a right hot mess today, Izzy," he said against those thick tufts of dark hair. "You need your sleep."

Sam watched the interplay, wishing Isabel hadn't turned her

face toward Henry's neck.

"Before I answer any more of your questions, Detective Chastain," Henry said, "I need you to answer one of mine."

"What is that?" Sam asked.

Henry's jaw clenched as his eyes burned into Sam's across the small room.

"How'd my baby, who disappeared from that parking lot up in Taos, end up right back here in Santa Fe?"

11

Cici

*All of my misfortunes come from having thought
too well of my fellows — Rousseau*

"I don't know," Sam said. His complexion remained ashen, his eyes sunk deep thanks to his near-sleepless night.

"What do you mean, you don't know?" Henry's voice turned hard and cold as night, making Isabel open her eyes and stare at her father, her lower lip quivering.

While Cici understood Henry's frustration, antagonizing Sam and upsetting the baby wouldn't solve whatever tangle they'd ended up in. Cici leaned in farther, nearer to where Henry now sat in the rocking chair by the crib and offered the baby the pacifier she'd used in the night to try to soothe her. Cici then reached out and rested her hand on Henry's wrist. His pulse jumped in rapid fluctuations, but he remained still under Cici's palm.

"About…I guess it was after eight, maybe closer to nine last night, my dogs became restless," Cici said. "Mona started sniffing the door."

Henry pulled his daughter closer. She spat out the pacifier and smiled up at him again. His soft return grin gave Cici pause. This man adored his daughter.

"Why did you call an ambulance then?" Henry asked. His pulse kicked up under Cici's fingers.

"To make sure she's healthy, safe," Sam said. "Also, it's protocol when we discover an unaccompanied minor."

Henry's eyes widened and panic crept across his face. "Did the doctors find anything wrong with Izzy? Has she been hurt somehow? I worried about that. About all the sickos out there who'd prey on a baby."

Cici patted Henry's arm. The man worked himself into a froth as he asked these questions. "No, she's not hurt. As far as I know," Cici said.

Henry turned to Sam, his scowl deepening. "And you, Detective? Is that what the doctor said to you, too?"

"It is," Sam said, his voice neutral.

Cici didn't know how Sam could remain so calm.

"So, why'd you wait until after ten last night to call me?" Henry demanded.

"Because we had to wait for the EMTs to check Isabel out to make sure they could move her before they put her in the ambulance. From there, she had to be admitted to the hospital. Also, I needed to let my boss know Isabel showed up at Cici's house and what I was doing to ensure her safety. Then, I called you."

Sam's answer seemed to mollify Henry somewhat.

"I also called Grace's number," Sam said.

"Oh," Henry's face collapsed inward, grief etching dark grooves around his eyes. "Did she ask about me, I mean…what did she say?"

"I left a message," Sam said.

He kept his voice devoid of emotion, and if Sam felt as Cici did, he struggled to do so. Henry clearly adored his daughter and his wife—but something had happened and it ripped them apart. The man was going to have to find the strength to put his family back together.

Cici wanted to be there for them as they worked through their issues.

If…Cici swallowed, trying to force the faint metallic taste of fear forming in her mouth. *If* Grace Bruin was still alive.

———

Isabel fell back asleep. Henry continued to hold her, rocking gently. After a while, Cici's eyes drooped again and she slid back into a light sleep, her head resting on Sam's shoulder. For the first time in days, Cici did not dream.

When a light knock came at the door some time later, Sam raised his head from Cici's and they both stretched and groaned.

Henry opened his eyes, blinking blearily, his big hands cupping the baby to his chest.

A woman Cici hadn't seen before popped her head around the door, her nervous expression easing when she locked gazes with Cici. She sidled into the room with slow, careful steps, a half-hearted smile curling her lips. She clutched a stack of papers to her scrub-clad chest, her eyes darting from Henry to Sam and back again.

"Good morning," Cici said. She had to stifle a yawn.

The other woman tucked her grizzled waves back behind her ear, the faint lines around her mouth deepening as she once again glanced at Henry. "Hi. I'm Lila Klein. I'm the social worker on staff here." She glanced back down the brightly painted corridor. "Um. I'm waiting for the security. He's…here," she said, her shoulders sagging a little.

"Is there a problem?" Henry asked, his voice rising. "What's wrong with Izzy? Did Grace cause a fuss?"

"I don't know anything about a Grace," Lila said, nerves making her voice squeak. "But…Isabel appears just fine."

Lila smiled down at the baby who snuggled into her dad's lap, playing with her toes through her thin socks.

"Excellent news," Cici said, her smile growing until she caught sight of Sam's concerned gaze flicking from Lila to Henry. Uh oh. He expected trouble.

"So, Isabel can be discharged," Lila said, her voice quavering a little. She swallowed hard. "But I…I can't discharge her to you, Mr. Bruin."

Henry gawped, his entire face slack with shock and hurt. Cici felt as though she'd been kicked in the chest by a donkey, so Henry must feel even worse.

"Why?" he managed to ask.

"We have a claim of abuse."

"What? Who said that? When?"

Lila looked both skeptical and sympathetic. Cici didn't know how she pulled that off.

"Until this claim can be substantiated—"

Cici made a choked noise. The mere thought of how scared little Isabel must have been during the entire ordeal, the idea of a parent having to live with that reality of their child vanishing like that and now claims of abuse…Cici shuddered, gripping her arms and rubbing her palms up and down to stave off the iciness seeping into her skin.

"I'd never…how can you think I'd leave my baby? H-hurt my…hurt my baby?" Henry's voice rose, billowing with anger.

"I can't share more information with you. We have a claim that must be reviewed, Mr. Bruin. It's protocol," Lila said, her voice filled with misery but also a finality of someone who understood her role. Her face reflected the same discomfort and steel will. The paperwork she held crumpled under the force of her shaking hands the only visible sign of her agitation.

"There has to be something you can do," Henry said, his voice pleading. His gaze darted around the room even as he snuggled Isabel closer to his body, hunching forward to protect her better. "Izzy needs me. She just got back….She'll be scared. We don't know what happened while she was gone. Why do you want to frighten my child?"

Lila drew herself up, her eyes flashing with the self-righteousness of her title and work. "We work to help children, Mr. Bruin. A police report was filed last month about the safety of the child in Taos."

"Would that be by my mother-in-law?" Henry snorted. "She hates me. She tried to get custody of my daughter before we left the hospital. Is that what you're talking about? Because it's bogus. I'll get a lawyer, do whatever, but I want my daughter home with me."

"We must make sure the home is safe for the baby," Lila finished, her eyes downcast now.

"So I'm guilty with no way to prove my innocence?" Henry asked, his voice tinged with bitterness.

"I didn't say that, Mr. Bruin," Lila said. "But you're asking me to believe you while another party is asking us to believe them. And a baby's well-being hangs in the balance."

Henry made a guttural sound. To Cici, it seemed he was trying to process both anger and grief. She understood both those emotions only too well.

"How soon can Henry prove he deserves custody?" Cici asked. "That he's a safe parent to Isabel. It'll be a hearing, right? And…" She wracked her brain for the correct terms. "The child services people will come to the house, make sure it's clean and… whatever," Cici finished lamely. She needed to be better up to speed on the process.

Lila tipped her head toward Cici. "Depends. There'll need to be visits. Some consultations with witnesses and those who can vouch for the safety of the child in the home."

"Her name is Isabel," Henry said, his voice shaking with repressed frustration. "She's a person, same as you, and you're intentionally scaring her."

"But he *can* prove it and he can get full custody of his daughter," Cici asked, turning to face Sam.

Sam nodded, but his eyes remained shadowed and a bit melancholy. Something dark and ugly reared up in their depths.

"And you can visit her, I bet, while this gets sorted out," Cici said.

No one moved. No one spoke.

Cici's palms began to sweat.

"Right, Sam?" Cici asked. "He can."

"We'll see what CYFD can do to facilitate that opportunity," Sam said, but his voice was lackluster. "Once the proper authorities know what's going on and Henry's deemed safe to be around the baby."

"So, you want me to…what?" Henry asked, his voice cracking. "You just expect me to turn over my baby to…to… child services?"

Lila's eyes filled with tears and she clutched the papers even tighter to her chest. "I'm sorry, Mr. Bruin. Really I am. But I have to follow protocol. For the child's safety."

Henry blew out a breath, but Cici could see how hard he worked to hold together his emotions.

"I told you, her name's Isabel," Henry snapped, his frayed temper obvious in both his tone and his dark scowl. He continued to cradle Isabel, who was still snuggled tightly against him.

"All right," Lila tried to soothe.

Too late for that one.

"Mr. Bruin, if you don't give her over, the police have to intervene. You could be charged with a crime." Sam leaned forward, his hands still linked between his knees. His knuckles turned white. "If that happens, getting your daughter back will be much more difficult. CYFD cannot release a minor into the custody of a person with a violent, criminal history."

The relative silence spun out and Cici struggled not to fidget. Her heart ached for Henry and for Isabel.

"Yeah." Henry cleared his clogged throat. "I understand."

Isabel sat up and patted Henry's cheek, her tiny hand a few

shades darker than Henry's pallid complexion. "Dada. Dada."

He cuddled the baby close, pressing his cheek to her forehead. Isabel waved her hands before finally latching on to Henry's short strands of hair.

"I don't want her scared," he murmured.

Isabel's first wail was soft and snuffly. Henry raised his head and pressed a soft kiss to the spot between her eyebrows. The baby kept her eyes glued to her father's face and repeated over and over her favorite word: *dada.*

Cici's eyes filled with sympathy tears when Henry's shoulders shook and he pressed his scrunched eyes against his daughter's soft neck.

12

Cici

To endure is the first thing that a child wants to learn, and that which will have the most need to know. —*Rousseau*

Cici stood, her legs shaky. "Sam, may I talk to you?"

He nodded, lips pressed together, and led Cici out into the hall. She leaned back against the wall and hugged her arms to her torso.

"Isn't there anything you can do to help him?" Cici asked.

Sam closed his eyes, as if unable to hold Cici's gaze. Or, maybe, he was too exhausted to keep his eyes open for another moment. He settled next to her and tipped his head back against the wall.

"This is the law, Cee." His voice was raspy and weighted with the same exhaustion that was also pulling at Cici. He opened his eyes and tilted his head down to look at her, his expression pained.

"You saw that man in there. He's hurting. He's not a freaking criminal! And this is ridiculous. CYFD leaves kids in homes all the time. I know because you've complained about it before."

Something clicked in her brain and she turned to stare at Sam. "You know that. You…you want Isabel out of her family house." She shoved her fingers through her hair and pulled.

When that didn't help release her frustration, she kicked at the plastic baseboard. Then, she shuddered because her toes throbbed.

Sam's tone remained too unfeeling for Cici's mood when he said, "Temporarily. Until he can prove he didn't abuse either his wife or his child."

Cici nodded. "You're playing with a child's emotions, Sam."

"I'm trying to keep her alive, Cici."

Cici clutched at the folds of her cardigan she'd collected last night before leaving her house. "I don't want them separated, Sam. Don't do this," she said.

"A gut feeling?" Sam asked, pushing off the wall, his eyes brightening as he blinked to alertness.

"I don't know…" Cici took a deep breath as she let the semiquiet of the early morning hospital seep over her. "Yes. It's… you know how I said Aci communicated with me before? Trying to give me information for Evan? So he knew she loved him?"

Sam dipped his head. "That helped us crack the case."

Cici swallowed, hoping Sam wasn't hurt again. Anna Carmen loved Evan, and Cici wasn't exactly sure what Sam's feelings for her sister had been, though for years, she assumed he loved her.

With Sam, she sometimes struggled to pinpoint what he was thinking, feeling—how he processed her comments. Which was strange because Cici made a living at gauging people's reactions and making sure she cultivated an appropriate response to their needs.

But right now, Sam was closed off, and she couldn't read him.

"I…I think it's like that again. That's why I had this dream about this family…I know it sounds ridiculous, but…well, why not? Aci knew that Isabel would come to my house. Like she wanted me to be prepared. To let me know this was bigger than just…well, a whopping lie about a baby being abducted."

Cici shuddered, wrapping her arms around herself to hold in her body heat.

"Who *does* that?" she murmured.

"Someone who's desperate," Sam said, his gaze drifting back to the room where Henry sat with Isabel, his frown intensifying.

Cici's mouth twisted. "You think Grace was so anxious to be with her daughter? No, *you* think Grace was frantic to get away from Henry so she kidnapped her own baby?" Cici allowed her words to drip with scorn.

Sam grimaced, his gaze drifting back to the door when Henry hugged his baby, his heartache clear for them all to see.

"I get you're pissed at me and at the system," Sam said, his voice hardened with resolve. "That you think it's unfair to separate the two of them. But I don't know what to think yet. I'm heading up to Taos," Sam said. "I'll talk to Grace. That's top priority." Sam muttered to himself, like he was making a list. "I'll need to talk to my counterparts, check into the family's background, find friends to interview."

"Which means you don't believe what I told you. Not really."

Sam blinked at her but didn't answer, giving Cici the response that set her belly full of fire.

"You know what, do what you gotta do. But in the meantime, can we make sure Isabel's with someone good over at CYFD?" Cici pleaded, understanding she wasn't going to get more from Sam concerning Henry's plight. "I just…she's been through a lot and so has Henry."

Sam dipped his head. "She'll go to emergency foster. Unless they don't have one, then it may be a staff member. They've all had their background checks."

"Not good enough. I want someone watching her that cares about her, Sam. Already. Who has a stake."

Sam clenched his jaw but he asked, "Who do you want me to talk to?"

Cici recognized this as an olive branch, and she appreciated the effort Sam chose to make with her. "Becky Gutierrez," Cici said. "She's always been on top of her work there."

No, her reason for asking for Becky was much more personal: Cici didn't think Sam would find her and this was her way to prove the point.

Sam tugged on his lip but he nodded. "You know I can't do that. Becky knows Grace. Henry said so."

Cici rolled her eyes as she exhaled. There were moments, like this, when being in a small city made everyone's life harder. "But I asked you to find her. She'll be able to help navigate the system and get Isabel into the best hands…after her father's."

"Cici—" Sam said, his voice dipping in warning.

Cici crossed her arms over her chest and glared up at Sam. "Isabel's been through trauma, and whether you like hearing so or not, your stupid protocol is going to increase it."

"I'll see what I can do," Sam muttered, his expression unhappy. "But you have to understand—again, this is for the child's safety. If Becky and Grace are related, Becky won't be able to oversee this case." Sam raised his hand as if to ward off Cici's next words. "Still, I'll call her to give her a heads up. That'll help establish a paper trail for Isabel. And, maybe, if Becky is as close to Grace Bruin as Henry said, we can get some insight into what happened last week."

Cici unclenched her fists, but her anger didn't abate. "*If* you find Becky."

Sam opened his mouth, but Cici held up her hand. "Go investigate. Do your thing. I'll do mine. But I want it on the record right now that I thoroughly and deeply oppose this decision."

"All right. Just…be careful." He raised his hand, palm out. He hesitated a moment, then said, "Call me when you leave here. I want to know where you go today."

Cici tamped down her irritation with a struggle. "Why?"

Sam stepped away, pulling out his notebook. He would focus on the case and do what needed doing to ensure justice.

"Because I want you to be safe," he muttered.

"Funny," Cici snapped, arms crossed over her chest. "I want the same thing for that baby in there—the one whose safety you're putting at risk."

Sam grimaced. Cici rarely picked a fight and she felt bad taking out her spiking anger on him. Still, in this, he was wrong.

"I'm off to Taos to find out why Grace Bruin won't return our calls." He spun on his heel and strode down the corridor.

But Cici already knew—and so did Sam, the stubborn goat.

"Remember what the note said," Cici called.

He glanced back and something lit in his eyes. "I'll be careful. And I promise not to trust anyone."

Cici frowned, wondering if he meant her.

13

Sam

Our earthly joys are almost without exception the creatures of a moment...— Rousseau

---

The drive to Taos took the expected hour. Because of the rain the night before, the temperatures were ten, maybe fifteen degrees cooler and Sam rolled down his windows, enjoying the faint rushing sound as the road neared the Rio Grande. A few yellow inflatable boats dotted the foaming white rapids. Sam used to love the rush of sliding over the rapids.

He and Cee should hit the river once her ankle healed fully, he thought. He brought the jumbo-size travel cup of coffee to this mouth. That was, if she forgave him for his lackluster response to the likelihood of Henry getting his kid back any time soon.

She was angry. Worse, she was hurt. Cici required time to forgive what she perceived as betrayals.

Not something he could worry about now. Instead, he made another call up to the police department in Taos, letting the receptionist know his approximate arrival time. He needed to speak with the detective that had worked the case there first to see how best to approach Grace and her family.

In the back of his mind, the note wrapped in Isabel's blankets niggled. *Isabel's not safe. We made a mistake researching those deaths. He must work for the police.*

Top that concrete piece of evidence with Cici's belief that Grace was trapped somewhere in a basement and the situation appeared dire. But Sam had to follow the evidence, and he'd already spread his meeting about this case across all three departments that housed criminal investigations. He'd taken most of the drive up here to speak to his boss about his concerns. The captain suggested Sam not forward the note or what it said just yet and instead get the lay of the land among the officers assigned to work with him on the case, assess who he could trust.

He pulled up in front of the sparkling glass-and-stucco building a few minutes later. He exited the car and stretched his arms high over his head in the hope of clearing his muzzy brain. Late nights never used to be such a problem. Now he understood why the older guys on the force tried to keep normal business hours. Granted, the SFPD's homicide division wasn't large, so only a few men were on that particular force and they worked the hours needed—which often included until after five in the evening.

Damn, he was tired. He reached back into his city-issued sedan and pulled out the cup of now-tepid coffee. Well, cold coffee was better than none.

He walked into the lobby, ready to make some progress on the case. Apparently, his counterpart wasn't available, so Sam snagged a chair and closed his eyes.

"Detective Chastain?" A booming voice said to him about fifteen minutes later.

"Yeah," Sam said, standing. He blinked back the blurriness

of the cat nap and stuck out his hand. The older, burlier man shook it.

"Detective Phil Hartman. Good to meet you. I hear you want to talk about the kidnapping of Isabel Bruin?"

"Yes, please. We have a new development in the case, and I wanted to be sure to loop back around, see what information you'd gathered."

"Appreciate it," Phil said, waving his large hand in a follow-me motion. Once back in the main station area, he led Sam over to a desk in the corner piled with file folders and a variety of other coffee-stained papers. "It's always a mess," Phil scowled. "Apparently, it's how I think."

Sam settled into the chair, wisely choosing not to say anything. Instead he sized up the other guy. Sam guessed early to midsixties. Probably used to play some sport but now spent too much time at a desk, chasing leads and eating fast food.

Philip muttered "Bruin" under his breath and finally pulled out a file folder with a ta-da flourish. "Kidnapping. Took the baby while the mother—Grace Bruin—was putting groceries in her car. Just snapped up the carrier and…poof! Gone. Happened in town, but because she's part Tiwa, we contacted the Taos Tribal Police. I worked with…" Hartman thumbed through his pages. "Right! Kent Rivera. Nice kid."

"We have her," Sam said, keeping his voice low as he leaned forward, gauging Phil's reaction.

"What?" Phil asked, surprise causing his face to go momentarily slack.

"The baby. Isabel," he corrected to her name. Cici would kick his butt for not considering the child's feelings.

Phil whistled, eyes widening. "After all this time? She's home with her folks? Shee-it. I don't think I've had a case close pretty like that. Wait." He gripped the edge of his aluminum desk hard enough for his fingertips to go white. "Is she alive?"

Sam nodded. He catalogued each reaction, all of which seemed in line with a police detective who'd been doing this work for years.

"Damnedest thing," Sam muttered. "She was dropped off on a doorstep of a preacher in Santa Fe last night."

Phil sat back in his chair, adjusting his black leather belt and slacks at his waist and shifting his bulk in the seat to get more comfortable. "I'll be. You notified the mother? Last time I spoke with her, when they were here at the station, Grace planned to stay with her mom, Esperanza."

Phil's conversation with Grace must be where Henry came up with the idea Grace planned to stay with her mother. "Tried. Last night and again this morning—twice. Got her voice mail. She hasn't returned my call. And the baby's not home with her dad. CYFD's involved."

Sam's mind went back to Cici's dreams. But that's all they were: dreams. Giving them more credence could mess up his investigation. Or help him solve the case—as they had the last one.

Phil's eyes narrowed. He tapped his pen on his desk. "That's strange. Real strange not to hear from the mom. Especially since you told her about the baby?"

Sam nodded.

Phil hauled himself out of his seat. "I'll call the county and the Pueblo."

"I already did that," Sam said. "I've got meetings with them both." He'd wanted to make sure they knew he was coming, and while that might give them time to coordinate a story, it would also make it much harder for them to hide evidence…or worse.

"Oh. Well, let's go, then," Phil said. "We can do this together. Save us all some briefing time."

Sam nodded when Phil said, "Then we'll take a ride out that way and figure out what's going on."

———

Sam asked to stop at Grace's mother's house before heading to the sheriff's department.

"This isn't my jurisdiction," Phil said, frowning at the small, weathered adobe-and-wood home. "It's county, but it seems like we need to find the baby's mama first thing."

No one was home. Sam fretted about that, but he didn't have a search permit to poke around, so he got back in his car and drove to the sheriff's department. A receptionist sat at her desk, speaking to a man in a neatly pressed tan uniform.

"Hello, Brenda," Phil said. "I got Detective Samuel Chastain with the Santa Fe Police Department here. He's following up on a kidnapping case here."

"Oh, dear," the woman said, her hands turning all flighty across her desk. "A kidnapping case you said? Not that poor little baby?"

"That's the one," Phil said. "Only one we've had far as I know." He leaned in, ignoring the man in the sheriff's uniform who glared at him. "They found her. Dropped on a doorstep up in Santa Fe. Don't that beat all?"

Sam frowned. The woman was flustered and obviously in need

of reassurance that the child was safe. Sam realized Phil had a bigger mouth than a cutthroat trout. Great. He'd been assigned to work with the town gossip.

Sam shifted from his weight, becoming aware of the sheriff's stare. Sam glanced up into a set of deep brown eyes as the woman exclaimed on how amazing that was. Silver-rimmed glasses framed his eyes and bushy gray-speckled eyebrows. His hair was shorn short, almost military in precision.

Sam put out his hand. "Sam Chastain."

He took Sam's hand in a firm, no-nonsense grip. "Sheriff John Milstead. You got real lucky if that baby just dropped on in."

"Don't I know it," Sam said, his tone laconic—one he used when he spoke to another officer. This man understood the law. John's posture spoke ex-military almost as loudly as his buzzed head. Sam guessed John to be about ten, maybe fifteen years older than he was, and about ten, maybe fifteen years younger than Phil.

"Whatcha doing up here?" John asked, leaning his hip against Brenda's desk.

"Trying to reach Grace Bruin. I can't get her on the phone and we have some questions about the child's safety. CYFD needs next of kin for the child until we can ascertain neither parent had anything to do with the kidnapping."

Though, since arriving, Sam was beginning to worry Cici's dreams were much more prescriptive of current events.

John sniffed, crossing his arms over his chest. His shirt was so starched, the sleeves barely rippled with his movement.

"Don't know much about the daughter—Grace—but

you're not going to find fit folk in Esperanza. She's got a few outstanding RO's and her father's got a record of D&D's. Plus, he's like a million years old now. He's on Pueblo lands. We'll have to alert the Pueblo if you want to talk to him."

Sam's heart sank. Dammit. He'd known this wouldn't be an easy case. Restraining orders and drunk-and-disorderlies. These folks were turning out to be like a good too many CYFD ended up yanking kids from. And, to make the situation more complicated, he was definitely going to have to deal with all three policing divisions.

"Yeah, I'm going to need to talk to both of them," Sam said. "You heard from Grace at all? Since the abduction?"

"Nope," John said. "The cousin was in."

"Becky," Brenda said, twisting in her chair, her face still showing concern. "She's a good girl."

"Well, I'd like to speak to Becky, Grace, her mother, and grandfather after I look over your files, if that's okay."

Phil smiled at Sam. "Of course."

"Let's start with the mom," Sam decided. "That's your area, right?" He addressed this to John. Damn, keeping jurisdiction straight might prove the hardest part of this case. "What are the restraining orders for?"

"Come on back and we'll talk more," John waved them toward a hallway. He spoke over his shoulder. "The most important development Phil and I know about in the Bruin kidnapping is that Esperanza Ahtone filed a temporary injunction up here in the Taos courthouse days after the baby was born."

"Henry, the baby's father, mentioned that. Said he would fight this new iteration, but it means the baby was placed in emergency foster care."

"In Santa Fe?" Phil asked.

"In the area," Sam replied, unwilling to divulge more. *He must be police.* Yeah, Sam heard the warning loud and clear.

John scowled. "Let's focus on solving the abduction, shall we, Phil?"

"What happened to the injunction?" Sam asked.

"It was granted," John replied. His frown deepened further as did the disappointment in his voice. "Not on the best grounds, either. Mainly, it seems the judge sided with Esperanza Ahtone's claim that Henry wouldn't raise the child in a home conducive to her—I mean Esperanza's—heritage. And that was a type of abuse."

"That's the claim?" Sam's stomach sank. If that's all CYFD had, there wasn't a reason to keep the baby from her father. "But there was nothing in there about him hurting Grace or the baby?" Sam asked.

John shook his head. "Not a thing. From what we came up with, Henry Bruin is an upstanding citizen. Don't know how he married into this cluster of a family."

The coffee sloshed in Sam's unhappy guts. Cici was going to be furious when she found out Sam supported the removal of Isabel on basically no grounds—even more so when she found out he made sure CYFD found the flagged injunction that was nearly a year old.

John shuffled back through some papers. "Yep. Here. There were three old—dismissed—restraining orders filed against

Esperanza Ahtone and Fred Ahtone."

"That wouldn't prohibit the state from allowing them to have custody," Sam said. "It's old."

"Should," John muttered. On this, Sam whole-heartedly agreed. "And she's got a better option in her father."

Phil, who'd followed Sam and John back, leaned closer to the papers as if they'd clue him in. "Fred is Grace's grandfather and Esperanza is her mother, Fred's daughter," Phil explained to Sam.

John shot Phil a heated gaze that Phil ignored. Sam took note of the growing disapproval from John as Phil snatched up more papers, reviewing them.

"What happened to those ROs and who were they filed by?" Sam asked.

John shuffled through the papers, licking his thumb every so often to turn the page.

"Ah, here we go," he murmured. "Looks like the paperwork was filed on behalf of Grace Ahtone by her aunt Gemma Gutierrez."

"Gutierrez?" He started to pull out his notebook, but then he remembered. His stomach felt like lead. "Wouldn't happen to be related to Becky—Rebekah—Gutierrez would she?"

John gave them the beady-eye. "If you knew they were related, why did you ask?" He slammed the file folder shut, muttering something about wasting his time. Phil grunted, stepping back.

"She works in Santa Fe. At CYFD," Sam murmured. "I tried calling her this morning, but her supervisor said she'd taken a couple of personal days."

Cici believed Becky dropped Isabel off at her house, but Becky hadn't come forward, which worried Sam. The whole situation bothered Sam.

Sam mentally added a visit to the Gutierrez home to his ever-lengthening list of people to visit. And soon.

No one was home at Esperanza's place the second time Sam went by, nor was anyone at Gemma Gutierrez's house, either. Phil drove Sam out to the Pueblo, where Sam met with Kent Rivera. The young man's broad cheekbones and thin lips couldn't hide the baby-fat of youth and Sam wondered how the kid was old enough to work as an officer. After another round of introductions and handshaking, Sam explained the reason for his visit.

Kent appeared stunned. "The baby turned up in Santa Fe?" he asked, eyes wide and reminding Sam of an owl.

"Yeah. Last night. I need to speak to Fred Ahtone."

Kent nodded, his eyes glazed. "I can't believe she's in Santa Fe."

"What?" Sam asked. "Why?"

"How'd she get there?" Kent asked, his keen gaze pinning Sam.

Kent understood the process even if he didn't look old enough to own a gun.

"We're working on that," Sam replied.

"No contact from the person?" Kent asked.

Sam shook his head. He'd been through this already with the other two men.

All of a sudden, he wondered why the sheriff was involved. Taos PD, the Pueblo had both assigned men on the force to handle the case, which was normal procedure. But involving the sheriff, who Sam was sure had many other activities to oversee, might have been overkill. Definitely felt like a step too deep. Not that Sam could go back now.

"None that I know of. You got something?" Sam asked.

"Nothing," Kent said. He glanced at Phil and licked his lips. "You gonna come with us?"

Phil snorted. "To visit Fred Ahtone? No, outside my jurisdiction. And from what I've heard, I'm glad for it. See you back in town." He slapped Sam on the back and dipped his head at Kent before lumbering out to his car.

"Well, let's go, I guess," Kent said, his voice full of…some emotion Sam couldn't place. Concern, maybe?

Kent grabbed some keys and led the way out of the small building. He drove an old Ford pickup down one rutted lane then another. Sam knew, from growing up in the region, that Taos Pueblo had two of the longest inhabited structures in the country—some said they were built more than a thousand years before and the yellow of the native adobe brick caused the Spaniards who arrived in 1450 to think they'd found the fabled city of Cibola.

"You been with the department long?" Sam asked.

"No," Kent said.

"You from the area?" Sam asked, trying to keep the frustration from his voice. Talk about the opposite of a warm welcome.

"No." Then, as if realizing his answers were too short, Kent said, "I'm from Arizona originally."

"Navajo?" Sam asked.

Kent's lips twisted in a sardonic smile. "Half. Grew up on the Hopi rez."

"How'd you end up in Taos?" Sam asked.

Kent took a left at a dirt road. Most of the roads in New Mexico were dirt. Sam had read somewhere that the high elevation and sharp changes in temperature made maintaining the pavement too expensive.

"Job."

Sam fell silent, unsure where to take the conversation next.

"What about you, Detective Chastain?"

"Sam, please. I worked in Santa Fe, then transferred up to a task force in Denver. We specialized in children, specifically sex trafficking."

"What brought you back to Santa Fe?"

"My best friend was murdered there." The sharp twist of grief caused Sam to catch his breath. Kent met his glance and they shared that look—the one that offered sympathy and under-standing. "I wanted to be on that case."

"Probably the most important one of your career."

"For me? Yeah. For the kids we saved in and around Denver? No."

"You miss it?"

Sam considered the question. "Sometimes."

Finally, after a few more turns, Kent pulled to a rocking stop in front of an adobe structure. Kent turned to face Sam. He opened his mouth to say something, then closed it and shook his head.

He exited the cab with care, approaching an elderly man sitting in a wicker rocking chair on a narrow front porch. The porch used to be painted the turquoise many homes in the area boasted—a color meant to keep away evil spirits. But now the paint peeled up in many places and was covered in a thick coat of grime in others so that little of the positive turquoise color showed through.

The man on the porch didn't look much better. He had two long, silver plaits that probably fell to his waist. His skin reminded Sam of a piñon-nut casing—dark and mottled. His eyes were like the allanite crystals Sam had found during a visit to Lincoln County as a small child—black and dull.

"Why are you here?" the man asked. His voice, though deep, held a quaver of old age.

"Hi, Mr. Ahtone. Uh, this is Detective Sam Chastain from Santa Fe. He has some—"

"I'm actually looking for some information on your grand-daughter, sir," Sam said, cutting the kid off. Kent blinked at him, his mouth open, but he shut it at Sam's flat look.

Fred glared back. "Both her and her mama's missing."

"You sure about that, Mr. Ahtone?" Sam asked.

"You think you're the first cop to come calling? How about my wife? My sister? They're still dead and you did nothing." He looked out over the dusty land, no longer bothering to meet Sam's gaze.

"Your wife and sister?" Sam asked.

"Prove you care. Otherwise, get off my property."

"I want to help you, sir. We have your great-granddaughter in custody in Santa Fe, and I need to speak with her mom, Grace."

Fred humphed before he leaned forward and spat on Sam's shoes. "She married that hunk of dung, didn't she? Forces her to stay up in that nice house in Santa Fe, never come to visit her family."

"You're saying Henry abuses his wife, Mr. Ahtone?"

The older man turned away. "I ain't helping you with nothing."

14

Cici

Our minds like our arms are accustomed to use
tools for everything, and to do nothing
for themselves. — *Rousseau*

Unable to focus on the sermon she needed to finish crafting for this Sunday's service, Cici finally gave up. She shut down her computer and settled on her front porch, sipping a microbrew. Tipping her head back, she watched the large white puffy clouds drift through the late-afternoon sky.

Cici settled deeper into the Adirondack chair's bright turquoise cushions. She'd sent a note last week to Mrs. Salazar, thanking the older woman for sewing them. Her chair had never been more comfortable.

Unfortunately, Cici's mind, though clouded with fatigue, wouldn't settle enough for Cici to relax and enjoy her view of the mountains and setting sun. Watching Henry hand over his daughter slayed her emotions.

She was bone-tired and more than a little angry at the world—especially Anna Carmen for dragging her into this mess.

Sam hadn't called or texted her. She'd expected him to let her know when he talked to Grace. The fact that he hadn't reinforced her belief that Sam couldn't find her…and that Cici's nightmares were true. So much so, she worried deeply that Grace was the dead woman from her nightmare.

She *needed* Sam to call her, update her on Grace's current status. And alleviate Cici's growing concern.

He hadn't.

The sun sank toward the far horizon and Cici took a long pull of her beer. She closed her eyes, thankful Isabel's removal from her father now lay in her past. Cici planned to work with Henry to make the separation between the two as short as possible.

"Thinking about the baby?" Sam asked.

She opened her eyes to find him, foot raised onto the first step and knee bent. He rested both hands on his raised thigh, gaze firm on hers, gauging her response.

At least he looked as tired as she felt. But then, last night hadn't been kind to either of them. Whatever he'd been up to in Taos today etched worry lines around his eyes.

"Of course. And Isabel's parents. How this trauma to them will impact them in the ensuing years."

He studied her face and Cici glared back.

"You're upset over this situation," Sam said.

"Yes, Sam, I am. You weren't there when the CYFD social worker came to pick up Isabel." Cici tipped her beer back again, wishing it would wash away the scene from her mind. It didn't. She set the bottle down with a thud.

"The baby screamed as soon as the woman—Yolanda—plucked her from Henry's arms. Within moments, Henry broke down sobbing."

Cici took a moment to regain her composure. "It was awful," she whispered. She didn't add that she was unable to comfort either of them and watching the separation hurt her in ways she didn't quite understand.

Cici sensed the pain of watching the family separated had something to do with Anna Carmen's death, but she'd shied away from examining the situation more closely. Everything about her sister's murder still hurt. No point in picking at the unhealed wound.

Sam settled into the chair next to hers—sans pretty, comfortable cushions because Mrs. Salazar only made Cici one stating, "*You don't want to give those sinners more reason to stick around, Reverenda. In and out. In and out.*"

Sam grabbed her beer from her grip. Before Cici managed a "hey!" Sam tipped the long neck back and finished off the bottle.

"I'll get you another in a minute," he said. "I was thirsty."

"No kidding," Cici grumbled. "Why are you here?"

Cici didn't mean to sound so grumpy, but she was upset with Sam. He hadn't backed her—backed Henry—like she wanted him to.

"Something you said bothered me."

Cici's lips quirked up because, while she was upset with the situation, she couldn't be angry that Sam wanted to do his job. That she understood.

"Just one thing?" she asked, her tone laden with snark.

"This week? Yes."

"I'm losing my touch," Cici mumbled, shaking her head.

"Why are you so upset about the split of the Bruin family?"

"I don't want to talk about that," Cici said.

She pursed her lips, debating between a flippant answer that would never satisfy Sam or the convoluted truth she failed to completely understand herself. With a sigh, she leaned forward until her elbows pressed into her thighs as she closed her eyes.

"I went out with a detective and a sheriff—even met up with the Pueblo crime officer who'd helped with the original abduction. I got to meet Fred Ahtone."

Cici turned her head in time to see Sam's scowl. He was clearly unhappy with that memory. "Basically, I wasted the day.

"I called Becky Gutierrez this morning. Before I went up to Taos. I didn't get her, so I thought I'd leave a message with her boss—let her know the situation with Isabel and Grace. Yolanda said Becky took her vacation time. Kind of all of a sudden."

He shifted in his chair before crossing his left ankle over his right foot. Clots of dirt clung to the bottom of his dress shoe. He'd traipsed up and down a mountain today, then.

"Did you find out anything?" Cici asked.

Sam rubbed his thumbs over his eyes. He let out a long sigh. "Nothing yet."

Cici was quiet, a million thoughts flooding her mind.

"Tell me what's got you so upset," Sam said, breaking the silence and causing Cici to jump.

She hesitated. This line of reasoning was less straight-up logic, thus less attractive to someone like Sam, who wanted to use reasoning in all his investigations.

"Lay it on me, Cee. I need a direction to move forward."

Cici pursed her lips again and turned to glare at Sam. His eyes were closed, his head tilted back. Yes, he was as done in as she was.

"One current theory I read about mental health is we only have so much Teflon."

Sam made a scoffing noise, just as she'd anticipated. "Sorry," Sam said. At least he attempted to look contrite.

Cici's eyes remained gritty and felt swollen in their sockets. For some reason, a compulsion built in her—like she had to tell Sam about this theory, *had* to make him understand.

"Not the actual material, but a coating we use to let the vagaries of the day slough off."

"All right," Sam said, not bothering to lift his head. "You mean resilience."

"If you prefer that term, sure. One theory is that when that Teflon's gone—it's gone. Not replaceable."

Sam opened one eye, turned his head and squinted at her. "Not following you."

Cici rubbed her palms up and down her jean-clad thighs.

"If a baby's removed from her parents in such a manner—literally pulled from the mother's breast or her father's safe arms—and given to another person hell-bent on revenge, that can mess a kid up forever."

"Ah," Sam said. He knit his fingers together and stared at her with dawning respect. "The child might lose all its Teflon in one fell swoop."

"Leaving us with a less capable child. One who can't always rise above or even cope with the situation at hand."

"But why do that to the kid?" Sam asked.

Cici grabbed the empty beer bottle Sam had set next to his

foot and tapped it against the arm of the chair.

"You tell me, Sam."

He raised his eyebrows but held her stare. Finally, he sighed. "You're really mad at me."

"Yes."

"I did what needed doing."

"No," Cici said. "You did what *you* thought needed doing."

Sam's phone rang, no doubt saving them from a fight. He listened, his face falling into even more haggard lines. He hung up and swallowed down what must have been a bitter taste.

"Becky's been reported missing."

That brought Cici's gaze flashing up to Sam's.

"What? When?" Cici asked, fear once again creeping its way up her spine. "I told you she visited Grace! Got Isabel out of that basement."

The ache in Cici's chest—the one that started with her dream of Grace chained and had grown much larger after witnessing Henry's shattered expression today—now ballooned. She struggled to take in air.

Something…something about Becky and Grace.

"No one's seen her since the day after Isabel was abducted."

With Sam's words, Cici lost the elusive thought.

"You're *sure*?" Cici asked.

"That was her mother," Sam said. "Gemma Gutierrez. I tried to meet with her earlier today but she was out. She was looking for Becky. Thought she might have gone up to visit Fred Ahtone."

"Did she?" Cici asked.

Sam shook his head. "Don't know. I'll have to check it out

ASAP. Fred's a mean old buzzard, though, so there's no telling. I'm going to sit down with Gemma first thing tomorrow morning. See if we can figure out what happened to Becky. I also want to show her the note left with Isabel."

"You didn't ask her over the phone?" Cici asked.

Sam shook his head. "Certain things are best done in person."

As a reverend, Cici understood. Body language and small nervous ticks usually told Cici more about a person's mood and mental state than their words. She mulled over what Sam had told her.

"Becky's short—like me—and has dark hair," Cici said.

Sam nodded. "I know. I pulled a picture of her before heading up to Taos. I have one of Grace, too." Sam tugged at his lower lip. "The last time anyone saw Becky was Sunday morning."

Today was Tuesday, supposedly Cici's day off. She snorted. So much for a down day.

"Oh," Cici whispered. "And Grace has long, dark hair, too."

"Exactly," Sam said, that frown line forming between his brows. "Which means I still have a lot of work to do," he said on a sigh. "And the officers up in Taos don't seem all that interested in helping me. Well, except Phil, but he's a gossipy oldtimer."

"Is Isabel safe?" Cici asked. "I mean, with CYFD…wherever they placed her."

"That's my next call." Sam held up his hand. "I already called once before I came over here, and Isabel was fine. Yolanda was getting her placed with an emergency foster. Right now, she's down in Albuquerque."

Cici's shoulders relaxed. "Why?"

"Because that's the biggest facility with the best security."

Cici wilted. "Oh."

"I want her safe, too, believe me. I've already let my boss know what's going on. That was my next call as soon as I heard from Sheriff Milstead." At Cici's blank look, he said, "He's one of the men I met up with today in Taos. I'm working with him and Phil Hartman and Kent Rivera."

Sam's phone buzzed. "Text from the sheriff," Sam muttered. He rubbed his eyes. "He says he has more information."

Sometimes, like now, it was clear to Cici how working a case like this one took all his energy. Much as she wanted to help him, she couldn't do much except offer him a safe place to rest his obviously overworked mind.

"You want to stay here while you take and make your calls?" Cici asked.

"Yeah, that'd be great."

He glanced up at her, his eyes filled with gratitude that Cici didn't feel she deserved.

"Thanks, Cee."

"I'll scrounge up something for dinner."

———

Sam strolled into the kitchen about twenty minutes later. "First call was from Phil Hartman, my new contact in Taos. He wanted to pass along a name—Veronica Ortega. She saw Becky this afternoon driving a white Honda out of town."

Cici waited.

"Problem is, Becky doesn't own a white Honda. At least we don't have a vehicle registered to her of that description."

"Oh." Cici pulled some bread out of her toaster oven. "What about Grace?" Cici asked, trying to keep her breathing regulated.

Sam inhaled before releasing a long breath. "A white Honda Civic is registered to both Henry and Grace Bruin."

Though she expected him to say so, the words made the visions all the more real…and menacing. Damn her sister. Cici didn't want to be a conduit to more pain.

"I'm looking into the car, trying to find it, match license plates. The normal."

Normal for Sam, maybe. The logistics of what he worked through to solve a case—the magnitude of time and research—shocked her. Instead of commenting, Cici continued preparing dinner, glad he was talking to her about this.

"I asked Gemma to collect samples of Becky's handwriting. I'll do the same with Becky's boss at CYFD. Forensics will work on it as the materials come in."

"How long does that take?" Cici asked.

Sam rubbed the back of his neck. "Santa Fe doesn't have a large staff, so much of their work funnels through Albuquerque. That means it can get bogged down. And since you think we have two women missing, not just Becky, I'd really like to get some answers."

Sam cleared his throat. "I, ah, I also called Henry and asked for some of Grace's handwriting."

"You don't like Henry at all, do you?" Cici asked.

From the corner of her eyes, she saw Sam roll his. He looked like he wanted to kick something. She could attest to what a bad idea that was—her toes still throbbed from her attack on the baseboard at the hospital this morning.

"It's not that I don't like him," Sam said slowly. "It's just... something about this whole situation, especially Grace's abrupt disappearance...it bothers me. A lot. Until I know more, I want to avoid a possibly dangerous situation."

Cici nodded.

"That could get the police department and CYFD splashed back in the papers...and not for anything positive," he said.

Yes, Cici understood his reasoning, even though she thought the argument was weak.

Sam's phone rang again. He answered it. "Detective Chastain," he said.

"Yeah?" Sam asked. His eyes sparked with interest. "A match? You're sure? Parked in the lot off San Francisco, got it."

15

Cici

Happiness: a good bank account, a good cook and a
good digestion. — Rousseau

Cici looked down at the steam wafting in a soft, slow curl from her dinner. Much as she wasn't sure she wanted to eat, she forced herself to pick up her fork and take a bite. The sauce was rich, the spices and garlic warm on her tongue.

She chewed slowly then took another bite. Sam picked up his fork and began to eat. Halfway through dinner, one of the dogs scratched at the back door. Mona whined before banging against the wood door, probably with her shoulder.

"We have a potential lead. One of the patrolmen is impounding the car now. I'll have to go check it out soon."

"Take some of the pasta home with you, please."

Sam pulled out a glass dish, not having to be asked twice. He seemed to enjoy her cooking, telling her often it was so much better than the cereal, sandwich, or fast food he typically ate.

"So, I need to ask. Do you think this is all…" She couldn't recall the term Sam had used before.

"A domestic dispute?" he prompted. "It was more likely before Becky went missing."

One of the dogs scratched at the back door. Cici rose, but Sam waved her back to her seat. Sam was kindest when he worried they were on opposite sides of an argument. And today they were. Because Sam had never seen the way Henry looked at Grace. He just couldn't be the evil man Sam thought him to be.

She considered possibilities as Sam opened the door and the dogs scampered in, Rodolfo less stiff today—and, in short bursts, almost back to his pre-surgery playfulness. He nipped at his sister's ear as the two ran into the living room to tussle. Within minutes, Rodolfo would seek out one of his beds—a new one Cici had added to the living room after his surgery—and flop there to recuperate from this frenzied fun, but for now, Cici's heart warmed at the sight.

As Sam made his way back to the table to grab his plate. He ate quickly while Cici replayed Sam's words in her head.

Cici pushed back her plate, no longer able to even look at food—especially the rich red sauce that covered her pasta.

"I didn't tell you," Sam said. "Grace's mom—Esperanza—she filed a claim to be Isabel's legal guardian. Since she lives in the county, Sheriff Milstead became involved in that case. But she, like Grace, seems to have disappeared."

"So the baby can't go stay with her grandmother either," Cici said. "Well, that sucks."

Because she needed something to do, Cici began clearing the table, and then pulled out her broom and dustpan.

"That leads me to believe this is much more than a custody fight over a child—and because I don't know who all the players are, I'm disinclined to trust anyone associated with Isabel *with*

Isabel's continued safety." Sam's voice was quiet, weighted with sadness but also a willfulness Cici rarely heard from Sam.

Cici's pulse thrummed in her neck, pulling them back around to her original question earlier about Sam not liking Henry. "I get it, Sam. At least I think I do. But you're saying you still *would* keep the baby from her father?"

Sam's mouth drew down and he crossed his arms over his chest. "Look, I get that Henry puts on a good show, appears all loving, but we don't know how he behaves when we're not watching. And the man clearly has a temper."

Cici took a deep breath and released it slowly. "You really think that's fair to her?" she asked.

Sam scrubbed his fingers through his hair. "After our conversation on your porch? No. But I also can't stomach the idea of allowing a child back into an abusive home."

"And you think I do?" Cici cried.

"I think you want to believe in fairy tales and a happily-ever-after for a family that's dysfunctional," Sam shot back, his own frustration boiling over in both his tone and the way he crossed his arms over his chest.

Cici stood taller, her eyes narrowing. "That sounds an awful lot like you lack faith in my ability to view human nature—and individuals—with any kind of neutrality."

"There are lots of things that you simply don't want to see," Sam snapped.

Sam's words lit into Cici's belly, causing it to flame in indignation.

"Are you talking about the problems Anna Carmen got herself

into? Are you really throwing my sister's choices in my face?"

Sam's head jerked back, but his mouth remained in a tight, harsh line.

"That's low, Samuel. I didn't know Aci decided to play vigilante sleuth—I didn't *live* here then. I didn't *want* to live here after my father destroyed my family."

"Don't try to make me feel guilty about your sister," Sam replied. His eyes gleamed with emotion.

"Fine! You were talking about Aci because you think it's my fault she's dead." Cici blinked, trying to hold in the tears.

"No," Sam bit out, a deeper anger lacing his voice. "I was talking about *Isabel's* safety."

"You saw Henry with his daughter today, Sam. How much he loves her," Cici yelled.

Sam bent forward, his nose practically pressed to hers.

"Just like my dad claimed to love my mother—when he wasn't angry enough to slam a fist into her face."

16

Cici

My birth was my first misfortune. — *Rousseau*

Sam paled. Clearly, he hadn't meant to say that.

No, as his eyes shuttered and his breath broke, Cici understood Sam *never* meant to share this deep, painful secret with her.

Cici's heart sped up again, but this time out of concern—for Sam but also for herself. He'd intentionally kept this from her—witnessing abuse. What else had he omitted about himself?

"Did he hit you, too, Sam?" Her voice came out ragged.

Sam now leaned against the counter, head dropped between his chin toward his chest. Cici raised her hand and laid it on his shoulder. After a deep breath, Sam lifted his head and turned to look at her, knocking her hand away in the process. The raw pain there sucked all the air from her lungs.

"Yes."

That single word caused tears to burn in her eyes and she shook her head, not to negate Sam's words but the image that built immediately in her mind: Sam, as a young boy, cringing back from his father's much larger fists.

"You think I'd lie?" Sam snapped. His mouth twisted in an ugly, unhappy grimace.

"No." Cici swallowed past the emotional shrapnel ripping at her throat. "It's just…when you were at our house, you seemed…" Cici trailed off. *Normal* made it sound like she was judging. *Happy* did, too.

He snorted. "Your mom knew. That's why she let me hang out so much."

Cici stepped back, as much to accommodate his need for space as because she feared what he'd do this time if she tried to touch him. People handled their demons in different manners. Sam never liked admitting he had any.

No wonder he had turned to criminal justice. He wanted to help others—ensure they didn't have his upbringing of fear and pain.

Bits of memories sped before Cici's eyes. She tried not to be hurt by the revelations, by his disdain for her desire to comfort him now.

She failed.

"And before you ask, Anna Carmen knew, too."

Cici's knees locked and her heart seemed to stutter. Her *sister* kept such a huge secret from Cici? To this day, Cici still believed she and Anna Carmen were close—that they shared most of each other's experiences and thoughts. Clearly, after the stream of revelations that kept cropping up, Cici was wrong in her beliefs. Because her sister lied to her—at least through omission—about Sam and about researching the opioid ring that caused her death.

That caused a new, deeper stab of pain she'd have to unpack later. Cici tried to swallow but her mouth and throat were too dry.

"I never knew," she rasped. "Never even suspected."

"I didn't want you to know," Sam snarled. His eyes blazed. "*Ever.*"

Sam was like a trapped, wounded bear. She wanted to placate, to soothe, but that just pissed him off more. So she scooted back until she hit the refrigerator, wincing at the slice of pain in her shoulder blade and hip.

"I never wanted you to see me as a victim. Too weak to take care of himself."

Her hand came up to cover her own heart, but the damage there was already done.

"Is that what…" Her voice caught. "You think that's how I'd view you?"

Sam's laugh was caustic. "That's how everyone views abuse 'survivors.' As victims who were too young, too enmeshed, too stupid, or too weak to get the hell out. That's *exactly* how Anna Carmen saw me."

Cici bit her lip, worrying it between her teeth. Their gazes met, clashed. If he worried Aci saw him that way, then Sam would never want to get involved with a woman who pitied him. His sense of self would dictate he walk away, no matter how much he desired or cared for her. She wasn't sure how to parse through this newest revelation, and it wasn't the most important one.

"Is that how you see yourself?" Cici whispered.

Sam turned away. "I'm going to head out."

No, he couldn't leave. Not now. She needed to comfort him.

"Sam—"

"Make sure you lock up after me. I'll let you know if I find anything more about the case."

"Sam, please don't leave. Not angry at me, at the world." Cici began to raise her hand again, wanting, desperate to touch him.

"I'm not angry anymore," Sam said, his voice soft.

"Yeah, you're getting it." He smirked a little but the sardonic humor faded quickly. "*That's* why I can't just hand Isabel Bruin back to her dad. I must *know* without a shadow of a doubt that Henry won't hurt her, not intentionally and not physically or emotionally. She's…she's a baby, Cee."

Cici's hand slid up to her mouth. She shook her head once, trying to negate the reality of Sam's words. Of what he could mean.

A baby.

Had Sam's father abused him from such a young age?

The bleak look in his eye made her think yes.

Her stomach heaved and she compressed her lips tight to keep the bile from ejecting outward. She couldn't spew her disgust at such behavior, not with Sam present.

She needed to be strong, to focus on helping him without reopening a wound that clearly never healed. If she failed, he might never come back. She'd lose the most precious relationship she had.

She might have already.

17

Sam

Everything is in constant flux on this earth. Nothing keeps the same unchanging shape, and our affections, being attached to things outside us, necessarily change and pass away as they do. — Rousseau

Sam fell back into his past, into the pain and humiliation, not just of his father's words but his fists.

"Men like that…it starts small. Isabel would think it was normal—that all kids are grabbed too hard or swatted that often. It's what she'd know. All she'd know."

His voice was soft, full of the pain of adulthood looking back, of misplaced faith in the adults who were supposed to love a child.

Sam's hadn't. Only seen him as another feather in his cap— one to be used and forced into a certain behavior. Once Sam's mother had left, the box narrowed further until Sam could never meet his father's expectations.

Not that Sam begrudged his mother's decision to leave. Grady Chastain had woken up mean and downgraded to vicious as the day progressed. The fact Sam's mother had escaped made Sam… not happy, though he understood. What Sam couldn't wrap his mind around was that his mother hadn't taken Sam with her—that she'd willingly abandoned her own child to save herself.

On bad nights, Sam would ask himself who did that? Anna Carmen had once told him that the most desperate of people would.

His mother had dropped Sam off at school one day and just kept driving. Her car had been found in Farmington two days later. Sam had overheard his father on the phone, yelling about the large withdrawal his mother made from a checking account.

"I won't let Isabel suffer from that," Sam said, his voice hard, his eyes glinting with determination.

Cici nibbled at her lower lip, which she did when she was afraid to speak. Knowing Cici, she was unable to negate the utter devastation in Henry's expression when his baby was taken from his arms. Sam could tell her how good an actor his own father had been, but Cici's compassion tended to outweigh the harsh realities of the world—at least the world Sam had always lived in.

While Anna Carmen swore up and down that neither she nor Cici were ever hit, Cici had her own history with her father. The ugliness there—the ease with which he moved on from Cici's mother to another woman, dropping his kids without even looking back—shaped the woman Cici had become. Just as it had her sister.

Cici suffered from neglect, not abuse. It hurt differently, and she'd sought a different type of career to help her soothe her own scars. At least, that's what he'd pieced together.

And like both the Gurule women, Sam, too, chose a career that stemmed from not feeling safe, not feeling wanted, by those who should have wanted and cherished them most.

"Even if that means hurting Isabel in ways we can't understand?" Cici asked, her voice soft but filled with the conviction of her own experiences. "In making it harder for her when she's sixteen and twenty-five and…and fifty to trust the people in her life who are supposed to care for her?"

Sam clenched his jaw and the muscle there jumped. He'd known this would be her line of reasoning. Anna Carmen used it before, too.

Still, Cici's words brought forth that rush of wanting to belong. That need to be loved. Sam fought hard to make sure no child went through that—ever.

"She's not you, Sam," Cici said.

No, Isabel wasn't him. She was still young enough to live a fulfilled life. One Sam wanted to give her—no matter what Cici claimed. "She's not you, either."

Cici bit her lip again and looked down. "You're right. But she deserves to be part of her family," Cici said. "She needs to be."

Family. Cici, Anna Carmen, and their mother had been his family. Until Sandra had asked Sam not to pursue a relationship with Cici, and everything had shifted.

Sam's lungs ached like they'd been compressed—between the rock and the hard place he now found himself.

"There are times when you really piss me off." He walked to the door and shut it behind him with a soft thud.

18

Cici

Those who distinguish civil from theological
intolerance are, to my mind, mistaken.— *Rousseau*

As a survivor of violence, Sam had to work out and work through what it meant to him that Cici now knew of his past. Her knowing would change his *perception* of how she viewed him, whether she acted any differently toward him or not. She clenched her fists. She wouldn't act differently, she promised herself, because Sam was her best friend—the one person who knew and understood her life before in addition to the life she was trying to build since her twin's death.

Cici normally spent a few hours each week at the penitentiary south of town. She'd seen just how perception of reality played out over and over among the inmates housed there—how their feelings of inadequacy or impotence toward protecting family members on the outside hindered their ability to rehabilitate and better function in that world where they were needed. And she'd watched those feelings destroy some marriages, too many families.

Sam's sense of justice was deep and didn't allow for gray. Not when it came to children. With this new insight into his past, Cici finally understood why.

Though, she wished she didn't. Cici let her dogs in, numbed by the realization that Sam's slip in the heat of anger—her new knowledge—might pull too hard at the fabric of their relationship for Sam to ever feel comfortable around her again.

When she climbed into bed that night, she wanted to weep for the child he'd been, for the man he'd become who thought he needed to hide that facet of his past. But her eyes remained dry and her sleep restless.

She dreamed of the dead woman again but not as her. Just of her being dead. Of the note pinned to her chest: *You're next.*

The next morning dawned hot and sticky—an unusual occurrence that set Cici's patience level at zero. After two cups of coffee and an abbreviated walk with Mona that left them both panting, Cici bathed in a tepid stream. She dressed, slowed by a deep longing to climb back into her bed. She picked up her phone and called Henry to ask how he was handling this new day. Before she finished her question, Henry burst into tears.

Unsure how to solve the issues with Sam or Henry, Cici climbed into her Subaru and drove to the Bruins' small house off of Agua Fria near Frenchy's Park. She sat out front with the air conditioning on full blast before she pulled her phone out and considered typing out a text to Sam.

He was angry with her, sure, but that didn't mean he wanted her in danger or hurt. She bit her thumb, trying to decide what was the best course of action.

If Cici was wrong about Henry, then coming here could prove dangerous. Sam had driven that point home many times over the years even before her most recent and terrifying run-in last month. Cici understood her twin's death was caused in part because she didn't share information with the people who could—and would—have helped her.

I'm at Henry's house.

Short, sweet. Hopefully, Sam understood all the emotional effort behind the text.

She shoved her phone back into her pocket and opened her car door. She stopped, one foot on the ground, the other still inside the car. No, Sam wouldn't. He'd see it and think Cici intentionally came here just to prove Sam wrong.

So before she went up the path, ignoring the sweat that began to prickle over her skin, she typed out a second, longer message.

I thought you'd want to know. I don't want you to worry, and, yes, I heard everything you said last night. But he's broken, Sam. I can't leave someone in need. Just like I can't stop thinking about you.

She reread her words and deleted the last sentence before hitting "Send." With a heavy heart and a heavier sigh, Cici trudged up to the front door.

When Henry opened the door, Cici's eyes widened. She'd seen the man a day ago, but he appeared to have aged decades in that time. His shirt—rumpled when he arrived at the hospital in the middle of the night—was now creased and stained with coffee and sweat. His hands trembled—Cici guessed from too much caffeine. His eyes were so bloodshot; there was no way he'd slept during the ensuing hours.

He pushed open the door and turned away, trudging down the hall without greeting her. Cici closed her mouth on the greeting she'd planned and instead followed him through the house. Henry had settled himself onto the white, wooden rocking chair in the corner of the nursery. Flashes of jaunty fuchsia cushions poked out the side of his bulk. He hunched forward while he clutched a soft, pink teddy bear.

"I got a lawyer, like you suggested." His voice sounded as if he'd swallowed a bag of rusty nails.

"Who did you call?" Cici had given him four names, though only three of them practiced family law.

"Shawn Houlihan is going to represent me. He said to tell you hi."

Cici nodded. "Good choice. He's the best in the city."

"I read up on the names. He was my first choice, first call. He said he could get me custody within a week or two, tops."

Henry raised his reddened, desperate eyes to Cici. "You think that's true?"

Cici patted Henry's shoulder, working hard not to wrinkle her nose at his burgeoning odor. "I've never known Shawn to overstate his capabilities in litigation. If he says that's doable, then I suspect it is."

"There'll be a hearing. I've never had to do a hearing before, Reverend. I miss Izzy," Henry whispered, pressing his face against the teddy's fuzzy stomach. "Shawn said I needed to pick myself up, go into work. That'll help prove my case—that I can provide for my baby. But…I can't. I…it's like she's disappeared all over again. And Grace…"

Tears built and pooled in Cici's eyes as Henry struggled to get himself together enough to go to work.

"Don't get me wrong," Henry said, wiping his wet cheeks. "Knowing she's alive is such a weight off my chest. But it's also… the waiting is *hard*. I want my baby girl home, with me, where she belongs."

"You still haven't heard anything from Grace, then?"

Henry's jaw set and his eyes narrowed. "Not one word. What kind of mother *does* that? Just waltzes off and doesn't even care that her baby's been found? I thought I knew that woman."

Grief hit each person differently—made them behave in ways outside their normal modus operandi. She, herself, was guilty of such behavior, which was why she didn't want to judge Henry for his reaction. And it's not like she could tell him of her dreams—explain that she thought Grace wasn't able to come home. That wasn't just because Sam would recommend against sharing her visions, but because Sam needed the time and space to work through his investigation.

He'd find Grace. Soon. Hopefully.

She pulled out her phone when it beeped to read Sam's text.

I'd tell you to be careful, but my guess is you'd ignore that advice, too.

Clearly, Sam wasn't going to budge on his assumptions about Henry, nor was he going to offer her an olive branch about his past. She shoved the device back into her pocket as she wondered if maybe she did need to get more involved and search for Grace herself.

She settled onto the pink-carpeted floor, shocked by the number of shades of pink in this room. Her own mother indulged her twins' feminine sides, but this was…wow.

"Did you want a girl?" Cici asked.

"What? Oh, yeah. I liked the idea of having a little princess to spoil. Like my Gracie."

He swallowed hard, his eyes once again welling.

Something in her mind clicked. A connection that Cici hadn't seen before. Almost as if someone *(ahem, Anna Carmen, would you please be more helpful in the day-to-day, here?)* nudged the likelihood into the light.

"Henry," Cici began. Her mind whirring with possibilities. "You said something that made me wonder about Grace and Becky…I know they were related, but were they close?" Cici asked, her heart beginning to slam against her chest.

"Oh, sure," Henry said. "Grace was closest to Becky out of all her relatives. Becky came around while Gracie was pregnant, brought some cute clothes for Izzy. They liked to sit in here and talk. They talked a lot."

A low buzzing built in Cici's ears and her head went light— almost as if something tried to unmoor from her consciousness. "About?"

Henry shrugged. "I don't know. Girl stuff, I imagine. And their genealogy. They wanted to go back a few generations, were looking into their extended family tree. That's how I knew Grace's family's been in the Tiwa tribe so long."

"Yes, you mentioned that. Were they serious about it?"

"Yeah. Becky would go to the library and come over with new bits of information. They'd gotten all the relatives organized up to Grace's grandparent."

"Did you see the work? Does Grace have it?"

Henry shrugged. "Becky normally came over and hung out while I was at work—especially for my overnights. Grace didn't like to stay in the house alone."

This led Cici to the question she'd wanted to ask—the one that popped into her head as soon as she walked into this room. Because Cici knew the answer. Did Henry?

"When was the last one? The last time they were together?"

"Um…" Henry scrunched his brows, thinking back. "I'd guess about a week, maybe a bit more, before Izzy's disappearance." He huffed a breath and squeezed the bear. "Yeah. I'd say a week before."

Yes, the women sat in here, this very room, talking. Cici blinked past the image, needing to ask another question—one with life-and-death implications.

"Did Becky go with you up to Taos? That day Isabel was taken? Was she there?"

"Grace called her, I remember…" Henry scratched the side of his head.

Henry raised his head, his bloodshot eyes fixating on Cici—much like a spider locks its many eyes on the fly stuck in its web. "Why are you asking me all these questions?"

"Um," Cici said, trying to calm her breathing.

But she couldn't answer more because the images she'd tried to blink back shimmered in front of her. The space around Cici seemed to bend and heat, like a strange mirage right there in the pink-and-white polka dotted nursery. Cici gulped but at that moment, the vision slammed into her mind.

19

Cici

Plants are shaped by cultivation, and men
by education. — Rousseau

She landed in this exact spot in this room. Except now, Grace
and Becky sat together, heads bent close as they ooohed over the
baby's chubby feet stuffed into ruffled socks.

"You shouldn't have told him," Becky said, sounding scared.

"I know that now," Grace responded.

"I didn't think he'd be so angry about us looking into the family."

Becky shook her head, her long dark hair falling from a central
part down both cheeks. Her hair was straight, almost blue-black, and
longer than Grace's by a good six to eight inches.

"I don't think he's angry. I think he's scared."

"Of what?" Grace asked.

Becky shrugged.

"I'm happier than I've ever been in my life, Becks," Grace said,
her light brown eyes smiling at her cousin's darker, richer ones. "I
want him to be happy too, you know? And my mom. She hasn't been
right since my dad drown."

Becky narrowed her eyes. "I told you, my mom said your dad's
death wasn't an accident."

"But how can we prove that?" Grace asked.

"I don't know," Becky said.

They sat, watching Isabel squirm and coo.

"Henry's treating you good?" Becky asked, touching the light bruise on Grace's cheek. "If you need to come stay with me…"

"I don't," Grace snapped. "I just need to figure out how to fix this one thing."

Isabel waved her fists and started to fret, possibly because of Grace's tone. Grace opened her mouth to talk.

Instead of Grace's voice, Henry's rippled over her consciousness.

"Reverend?"

———

"Reverend?" Henry called, his voice rising in panic. "I don't know what to do," he cried.

Sam's comments last night swirled through Cici's head. Could she trust Henry? Maybe Sam was correct and Cici shouldn't have such blind faith in the human spirit. Her identical twin sister was buried because she, too, trusted people she never should have.

Cici sat up, frowning as she lifted her hand to the back of her head, wincing at the goose egg forming at the base of her skull.

"What happened?" she asked, dazed and vaguely nauseated. Her lips were dry, her mouth a desolate wasteland in need of water. Whatever just happened, it was *not* natural. Her body continued to rebel. Cici wanted to close her eyes and sleep for about a year.

"She woke up," Henry said on a sigh. "Here."

Henry pulled a phone away from his ear—a phone that…was

that Cici's case? He thrust it at Cici. She fumbled but the phone fell to the floor.

"Who is it?" Cici asked.

Henry leaned forward. Cici shrank back but Henry stared into one of her eyes then the other.

"That detective, Sam. He wants to talk to you."

"Ugh. Not now," Cici said. Her head ached. Her eyes wanted to fall out of their sockets.

Henry leaned in even closer and Cici yelped. "What are you doing?"

"Pupils are the same size," Henry muttered. "Can you stand?"

He rose to his feet, giving Cici enough space to take a deep breath. Henry held out his large hand and Cici stared at it, the feelings from the two women in her vision washing over her. Grace's face was bruised and achy. Becky worried Henry had hit Grace. That emotion had come through strong then, and it reverberated through Cici now.

Cici scrambled up the wall.

"I need to go," she murmured. Her breath broke like she'd run a sprint.

"You look awful pale, Reverend. I think it'd be a good idea for you to take some water and rest a minute."

Cici tried to still the quivering working its way up her legs.

"Nah, that's okay. Um, would you pick up my phone?"

Cici pointed at the phone next to her right foot. Henry bent down and retrieved it.

"Here you go. It rang just when you fell over. I saw Sam's name on the screen and answered it." Henry peered into her face.

"Sam?" Cici replied. Wait. Henry had said that before. Cici placed the phone to her ear. "Hello?"

Nothing.

She pulled the phone away and squinted at it.

"He said to make sure you don't have a concussion. Can you turn your head both ways? Any nausea?"

Cici bolted toward the door.

"Where are you going?" Henry called, charging up behind her as Cici bee-lined toward the front door. "You can't leave. You might be hurt."

"I'll call Sam back in a minute, let him know I'm fine."

Henry reached the front door a half second behind Cici. His large hand came over her head and slammed the door shut. Cici cried out.

"I'm going to have to insist you take a seat," Henry said again, his voice sharper than she'd ever heard it.

Cici's heart stuttered, then rammed against her chest. She sat on the nearest flat surface, which thankfully, was a wooden bench. Probably where Henry took off his muddy or snowy boots in the winter.

A vise gripped Cici's lungs, forcing all the air from them. Black spots danced in front of her eyes.

Grace hadn't answered any of the phone calls Sam had made.

Sam's warning…the white Honda parked near downtown… Why downtown?

Both Cici and Sam thought Grace must be dead. And…and now, thanks to that awful vision, she had to wonder if Henry was the most likely suspect.

Cici covered her hand with her mouth to stifle her gasp, not wanting to bring attention to herself. Grace had disappeared *with* her baby to Taos just days after that conversation here, in this house, with Becky. The conversation where she was going to fix that one thing.

The thing being Henry? Leaving him?

But that didn't explain her vision of Grace chained up in Taos. Could Henry be keeping her there?

Oh, dear Lord in heaven. Sam had told her—she'd been blinded by the man. Did he even care for his daughter?

"Hold tight there while I get you some water," Henry said, his voice still commanding.

Cici nodded meekly. Henry disappeared around a half wall that separated the kitchen from the main living space. He turned his back to pull out a glass.

Before Cici could second guess herself or offer up an explanation to Henry, she bolted to the door, flinging it open as she pelted toward her car. Once inside it, she locked her doors and managed to start the ignition after two fumbling tries.

20

Sam

In all the ills that befall us, we are more concerned
by the intention than the result. — Rousseau

His phone rang, pulling him out of a dead sleep. Cici's shattered expression from the night before haunted him, but Sam knew, deep in his bones, he was doing the right thing for Isabel. Cici would get over it. But knowing that hadn't stopped him from battling his sheets and slamming his fist into his pillow for hours.

"Chastain," he barked into his phone, groggy. The first hints of gray light seeped around his blinds. He glanced at the clock. Just after four-thirty. He flopped back against the pillow with a groan. A paltry handful of hours' sleep for the second night in a row.

Now that his brain began to function, he immediately began to worry Cici wouldn't get over his storming out last night. She might not forgive him—or want to hang out with a loser victim like him.

"Detective? It's Damian. We got a body."

Sam's mind stopped, clicked on the word. Body. A homicide. "Woman?" he asked, but he already knew. Cici and her goddamn dreams.

"Yeah. She's ah…she doesn't look too good."

"Where are you?" Sam asked.

"Behind the Five and Dime."

On the Plaza. Cici's dream coordinates proved accurate. Sam scrubbed his hand over his face, wishing his eyes weren't so gritty.

"Be there in fifteen."

"See you then, Detective."

———

Sam threw on some clothes and hurried to the scene, his lights and sirens loud in the still-quiet streets. Not even the tourists were awake, queuing up out front of Café Pasqual's night-darkened windows. Sam checked the clock on the car's dashboard. Just after five in the morning.

Sam rushed toward the yellow crime tape, stepping over the first piece and under a second, his gaze scanning the area. There.

The body lay sprawled across the pavement, inches from the large, peeling dumpster that dominated the alley. Whereas the Five and Dime's storefront sat on the Plaza, its stucco exterior inset under the multi-foot overhang lined with freshly stained wood, the rear exit to the store fed into a narrow, grimy alley. Just like you'd find in any other city.

These moments, Sam could almost forget he was back in his home town. Staring at the inert body of a young woman, the dark pool of blood under her that soaked through her T-shirt and jeans, he could be back on the task force in Denver.

But he wasn't, and this murder happened mere miles from Cici's house where she'd dreamed of it so recently.

"Any identification?" he asked.

"No, and we haven't moved her yet," Damian Goodson said.

His hand rested on his gun, his face falling into a perturbed grimace. "I called for backup as soon as I found her. We're waiting for the photos."

"What tipped you off?"

Damian swallowed back a gag. "The coyotes."

"Howls?" Sam asked.

Damian nodded. Typically, the canines avoided the city center, but nightlife was not part of Santa Fe's charm and by eleven, most everything in the city shut down. By twelve-thirty, the streets were deserted, quiet. Perfect time for predators and scavengers to prowl. The fact they hadn't found her until around dawn gave Sam pause.

The Plaza typically began to bustle around nine in the morning.

"Any marks?" Sam asked.

Damian shook his head again, his complexion waxy. "From the coyotes? Not that I could see."

"FDMI?"

"Dispatch radioed they're on their way," Damian said.

Sam nodded. New Mexico had an office for medical investigations based in Albuquerque—where every autopsy in the state was performed. Under the main Medical Investigator were Field Deputy Medical Investigators, typically shortened to FDMI. Since this death occurred in Santa Fe, the FDMI would arrive in the next hour or so to do a detailed analysis of the scene. From there, the body would be bagged and tagged and transported to the state-of-the-art facility at the University of New Mexico in the heart of Albuquerque.

"Anything I should know?" Sam asked, walking toward the body.

"She's wearing a note," Damian pointed.

Sam crouched low, noting the red that had seeped into the edges of the paper. He squinted to read the bold, capital words written in black ink.

You're next.

"No purse, phone?" Sam asked. "Rings, earrings? A necklace, perhaps."

"Not that I saw," Damian said.

"Okay. Let's start a sweep through the parking lots and meters on that side of town and narrow down which car could be hers. And let's get all the garbage cans back here and in a"—Sam considered—"I'd say a four-block radius checked."

Damian stifled back a groan. None of the officers liked picking through trash. But there was always a chance the killer had dumped the victim's possessions nearby.

The SFPD's new forensic photographer showed up and began snapping pictures. Sam stood nearby, keeping an eye on the woman as the sun rose and his team did their job.

Damian thrust a Starbuck's cup into Sam's hand.

"You looked like you needed that," Damian said.

"Did." Sam took a deep gulp, ignoring the heat searing over his tongue and the roof of his mouth. The FDMI team waltzed into the alley. Another hour of work here at least. He itched to head up to Taos again, but something held him in place.

"We organized the trash. It's in the back of the patrol car that I'll drive back to the station. I'm off duty now. Let me know how this one goes." Damian looked back at the body, his mouth curled in concern. "She looks young."

"They're all too young to be shot with a .45," Sam muttered.

Damian nodded. "She seems familiar."

Sam turned to him, eyebrows raised. "Yeah? Got any guesses?"

Damian shook his head, still eyeing the body. "No. Not really. Hard to tell with her face so…"

Sam slugged back the last of the thick, rich brew. "Thanks, man."

His phone pinged as Damian walked away. Sam pulled it out, his stomach rolling and plunging when he saw Cici's name. *I'm at Henry's house.*

Why wasn't he surprised? And he wasn't. He'd known, deep down, that she'd go there today. It's part of what made him so angry—her insistence that Henry was good, redeemable.

Grady Chastain was none of those things. Even Cici could never make him into a decent man. Not that Sam wanted his father to…aw, hell. He shoved his phone back into his pocket, annoyance sharp and hot as it sizzled through his blood.

The phone pinged again, and he couldn't resist seeing what else Cici wrote.

I thought you'd want to know. I don't want you to worry, and, yes, I heard everything you said last night. But he's broken, Sam.

So was Sam.

Wait. No, he wasn't. He shoved his phone back into his pocket once more. He was not affected by his piece-of-shit father's actions.

He leaned back against the wall and stared with fierce

concentration at the field inspector as he rolled the dead woman to her side, no doubt checking the exit wound. Sam moved closer, thankful when the battle in his mind was silenced by the sight before him. He clicked over into observer mode, a great trick he'd learned young—yes, because of his father. Don't let the words hit their mark, don't react. Saved Sam a lot of pain and made his father lose interest.

For a time.

"Get what you need?" The examiner asked, glancing at the photographer standing behind him, lips white and face a faint shade of avocado. An older man, probably an artsy photographer who'd decided to try his hand at a traditional job with real health benefits. They'd had a couple of those folks before Justin had taken over the role. None lasted long, unable to stomach the gore and unwilling to work the hours the job demanded. This guy appeared on the same trajectory.

No one stuck around.

Even as he thought the words, he knew they were a lie. Cici stuck around. So had her twin. Well, until she hadn't. But Cecilia Gurule was constant to those she cared about. It's what had first drawn him to the girls—their unshakeable bond to each other. A kind of deep-seated knowledge they were not just loved by the other but protected. Always.

The examiner grunted as he lowered the woman back down. He picked up his clipboard, ignoring the smears of red on his gloves as he began to mark off his checklist.

"Ah, shit," Sam said, his voice grim as terrible feelings of anger and helplessness blossomed inside him. At least these weren't related to Grady Chastain.

Sam stared at the small pink plastic object laying to the right of the woman.

A pacifier must have slid from the woman's front jeans pocket and onto the dirty black asphalt. It lay, taunting Sam, just inside the white chalk line.

21

Cici

I would rather be exposed to all their torments than
be obliged to think about them in order to protect
myself from their attacks. — Rousseau

Glancing into her rearview mirror, Cici made out Henry illuminated in the doorway, shoulders hunched and a deep scowl blackening his features. Cici shivered as she pressed on the gas pedal and shot down the street. Two blocks to the north, Cici pulled over and opened her door just before she upchucked her two cups of coffee and banana from earlier that morning. She pressed her clammy cheek against the car's upholstery, hating the heat that clung to everything in a miasma of hate.

Her air conditioner made small headway against the humid air. Cici didn't understand how people lived with such bathwater conditions all day for months. The few hours of humidity made everything seem a million times worse. She forced herself to sit up and slammed the car door shut again.

Nope, not quite ready to move. Her stomach heaved again as the emotions Anna Carmen channeled slugged into her midsection.

With a groan, Cici leaned her head back against the rest.

To borrow her mom's phrase, Holy pinochle. Cici hated these visions even more than the dreams.

Perhaps it was the newness of the moment that left her so shaken. Much as she wanted to believe that, she couldn't. Because the interaction she'd just witnessed between Grace and Becky confirmed Sam's own gut instinct. One Cici obviously needed to heed.

The Henry Cici observed at his wedding and the other days at her church appeared to be a loving father and husband. But maybe Becky knew better—maybe she'd collected evidence that Henry had been hurting Grace and had planned to use it to take Isabel from him.

Cici needed to get to Sam and tell him that under the layers of makeup Becky wore, she had a thick dusting of freckles along her jawline and neck. Cici wouldn't have ever known about those freckles if she hadn't just shared that intimate moment with Grace and Becky.

A moment, Cici now worried, would ensure Becky's death.

Cici's stomach gurgled with unhappy intent but there was nothing left in her to upchuck so she pulled away from the curb and continued to drive toward her church office. She didn't know where else to go. Not with things weird between her and Sam.

Her fault. Cici shuddered, gripping the steering wheel as she realized she couldn't—wouldn't—leave the tenseness between them.

With a flick of her blinker, Cici turned on the next street and directed her car south, toward the police headquarters. Another place she hadn't wanted to visit—not since Sam had hauled her there after she'd been checked over at the hospital. He'd collected her statement and pretended he'd never kissed her, his hands firm on her hips, fingers digging just enough into the skin there to tell her he wanted more.

Yeah, his ignoring that moment...that's what hurt the most.

———

She pulled into a parking space in the police headquarters' lot and stared out her windshield. With a sigh, she put her car into park and pulled the keys from the ignition. Cici tugged herself out of her Subaru and walked up the front steps.

"Hi, Jen," Cici greeted the receptionist, who smiled and opened the plexiglass window as soon Cici walked up. "Sam around?"

"I haven't seen him." Jen scowled. Then, she leaned forward. "But, then, it's barely eight."

Cici glanced at the clock, shocked by the earliness of the hour. She felt as though she'd lived through multiple days in the few hours she'd been awake. "Tell him I stopped by, will you?"

"Sure thing, doll." Jen slid the plexiglass barrier back in place.

Cici turned away with no clear destination in mind. She refused to sit in the church office alone. She considered her options as she climbed back into her car and pulled her sunglasses from their case in her console.

Much as she wanted to go home, hop on her Harley, and ride until her arms ached and her gas tank hit empty, that wouldn't solve her current issues. She glanced at the clock on her phone. She didn't need to be at the church today until early afternoon to let in one of the community groups.

With a long, deflated sigh, Cici pulled out of the lot and

ALEXA PADGETT

headed toward the cemetery. She drove through the green wrought iron gates that led into the narrow, gravel road.

A few larger cottonwoods lined the sides of the gravel, interspersed with some well-shaped ornamental fruit trees. The rows of grave markers were also neat, though they showed a variety of materials and sizes. Cici headed over to her mother's grave—which was a pretty white marble marker about eighteen inches tall. Cici stepped from her car and walked over. She pressed a kiss to her fingertips that she transferred to the cool stone.

"Hi, Mom. It's been a rough few weeks." Cici stared down at her brown pumps, now covered in a thin layer of the ubiquitous Santa Fe dirt. The leaves of the tulips she and Anna Carmen planted about five or six years ago had faded and crackled in the heat of the summer sun. The wilting increased Cici's sadness.

"I should have brought fresh flowers. I will next time." She cleared her throat before launching into the whole, sordid tale. "Sam won't listen to me about the dreams, and I'm concerned it's all building to be too much. How can I get back on a good track? I don't just mean with Sam…I want to save lost souls, not bring the worst of humanity to justice."

Of course, her mother didn't reply, nor did she send down a divine message. Cici pressed her palm flat against the stone before shuffling the few steps over to her twin's dark granite marker.

"Guess you heard all that, Aci. I'm appalled I was so wrong about Henry. I really thought he was one of the good ones…"

Cici crouched down, clearing a bit of leaf debris that the wind blew up against the gray granite. The thick lump of emotion swelled in Cici's throat, making it nearly impossible to breathe.

"I'm so angry with you," Cici managed to choke out. She had to swallow a few times before she could continue. "If you're going to drop these little awareness bombs on me, I want you to know, I've missed you from the moment I went away to college in New York. You're not just my best friend, you are my other half, and waking up each day, knowing I can't talk to you, is such a harsh weight to carry. And I'm also so *angry* because I'm just learning how much of yourself—your life you kept from me."

The wind changed direction, drifting over Cici like a warm caress. She smiled a little and swiped at her damp eyes.

"That hurts," Cici whispered. "Those secrets. They hurt so much."

She swallowed down more of the resentment that wanted to choke her—time to process that later. For now, Cici had a selection of items to focus on.

"You should have told me about Sam's home life. I…I hate what he went through. I hate that I wasn't there for him, when he needed me just like I wasn't there for you that day at the Santuario. And before. Dammit, I've been a really *bad* friend and sister."

"I'm going to have to disagree with that statement."

22

Sam

*Virtue is a state of war, and to live in it means one
always has some battle to wage against oneself.*
— *Rousseau*

Cici stood and whirled, her hand raised to her heart. She
staggered a few steps before righting herself against her mother's
tombstone.

"Sam. Crap, you scared me."

Sam shuffled in closer, not so much in her personal space as
just near enough to catch her should she keel over—still a possibility with as pale as she'd turned.

"You have every right to be angry with me." Sam looked over
her shoulder. While he needed to be honest, the chafing against his
pride made him unable to meet her gaze. He shoved his hands in
his pockets, his shoulders hunching forward in a protective gesture.

"I was worried you'd think less of me. Anna Carmen said you
wouldn't. We had a couple of big fights about it, actually, but I
made her blood swear never to tell you."

"Blood swear?" Cici said.

"We both pricked our pointer fingers and smeared it on a
piece of paper. She refused to touch her blood to mine."

"Anna Carmen hated blood," Cici muttered.

She did. She hyperventilated and passed out more than once when she scraped her knee or if Sam took a hard hit in football.

"We only made one blood vow in our lives," Cici said, her tone thoughtful. "Strangely, it was at her insistence. Our father had left our mom for KaraLynn a few weeks before and Anna Carmen wanted to promise we'd take care of our mother, each other." Cici buried her face in her hands. Her breathing came in choppy spurts.

Didn't take a detective to guess why—Cici felt she'd failed her sister in that promise.

"What your father did, that's on him," Cici said, her voice firming with assurance as she spoke. "*He's* the one who will have to answer, if he's lucky enough, to God. But I don't think he'll be that lucky. I can't believe that. Not of a man who hit a child."

Sam flinched, hating the way she said those words, directing them toward him.

Cici worried her lower lip. Up until today, Cici had never censored her words or behavior. At least Sam didn't think she had. Nor did he want her to. His throat ached and his stomach heaved at the thought of losing the most important person in his life.

Sam lifted her limp hand and pressed it to his cheek. He inhaled hard as his eyes slid closed. He didn't speak—didn't know what he would say.

She kept her hand there, against his unshaven jawline, even after Sam dropped his own away. And, for a brief flash, Sam felt hope.

"I had a vision. At Henry's," Cici murmured.

Sam frowned. His eyes opened and his gaze pierced into her warm hazel ones. Cici let her hand drop away.

"Another one?" Sam asked.

"Yes. In my vision, Becky saw this big bruise on Grace's cheek. Becky wanted Grace and Isabel to come stay with her," Cici said, her voice dripping with regret

Sam worried at the corner of his lip. After a long moment studying her face, he said, "I'm going down to Albuquerque later today. For an autopsy. We found a woman. Behind the Five and Dime. Just like you said."

Sam could tell Cici didn't want to imagine being in that room, watching the medical examiner work, as her whole body shuddered, hard.

"Do you know who the dead woman is?" Cici asked.

Sam shook his head, trying to tamp down the frustration he felt emanating from his skin in thick waves. "She's battered. I'm afraid we'll have to look into dental records for a match."

"Did she have freckles?"

Sam frowned, pulling up an image of the dead woman. Finally, he shrugged. "As I said, she's been battered."

"In my vision today, Becky had freckles. Lots of them on her cheek and jawline."

"Then we'll have to look into those identifying markers."

Sam hesitated, wrestling with his thoughts. Cici waited, always patient with him, knowing he struggled with the idea of Anna Carmen feeding her information. The entire possibility still went against Sam's logic-driven mind.

"Do you think it's Becky?" Cici asked.

Sam pursed his lips, considering the possibility. "I really don't know."

"From my vision, the intensity of emotion—the worry over Grace talking to someone….a man," Cici paused, seemingly trying to collect her thoughts. "Yes, a man and it had something to do with a…a secret, maybe?" Cici groaned. "I don't know all the details. Aci kinda sucks at passing along usable information."

Sam's lips set in a grim line as the thought he'd been trying to push away finally breached the surface: one of those women Cici kept connecting with had run out of time.

23

Cici

To live is not to breathe but to act. — Rousseau

Cici's phone chimed. She whipped it out of her pocket, recognizing the ringtone reserved for church-related activities. She groaned as she ran a hand down her cheek.

"I need to open the church for the knitting club. Oh! Right. We moved the day. It's also senior yoga."

Sam dipped his head in acknowledgment. "I'll follow you there."

Cici trudged back toward her car. Once inside the sizzling interior, she started the vehicle, rolling the windows down in hopes of catching a breeze before the air-conditioner kicked in. A faint scent of sun-ripened apricots filled the air—rich with sugar and a pleasantness Cici could not equate with the knowledge she'd be back here, at this cemetery most likely, to attend either Grace or Becky's funeral.

With that depressing thought, Cici drove back through the gates and turned toward the north. The Sangre de Cristo foothills were dappled in shadow, thanks to the big, benign puffs of cloud moving in across the mountains behind. With luck, they would see some rain and a reduction of temperatures.

Sam stayed a couple of car lengths behind Cici the whole way back to the church. His presence remained comforting, familiar, even if she didn't know what to think of their current personal relationship.

She unlocked the church's main doors moments before the large, loud gaggle of women in the knitting group showed up.

"Hi, Cici," Hannah Ross called.

Hannah was by far the youngest member of the knitting group—a graduate student working on her degree at St. John's College. She bounced over, her long curly brown hair bobbing around her shoulders. She grinned, her eyes alight as she headed toward the doors.

Cici tried to return the smile, but it felt wan.

"Hannah," Sam called from the parking lot.

Hannah's smile widened and she turned toward Sam. She tilted her head and edged in closer. Cici walked into the building, leaving Sam and Hannah outside.

She went to her office and turned on the lights, after which she settled into her chair and began to peruse her emails.

Sam strolled in a few minutes later and plopped into one of Cici's new visitor chairs. Cici purchased two new low-profile leather club-style armchairs after Sam complained about how uncomfortable the wooden ones had been. They'd been her first expense outside her vestments and she had to admit, she loved how they looked.

"Why'd you leave?" he asked.

"You seemed to want to talk to Hannah," Cici said, still staring at the computer.

"I did."

"That's why I left."

Sam's sigh nearly shifted the papers on her desk. "What's gotten into you?"

Cici pushed back from her desk and glared at him.

"Oh, I don't know. The fact there's another dead person in my town. The fact someone left a baby on my front porch. The fact my dead twin is sending me visions of abuse. Or maybe it's that you lied to me. And you refuse to believe me about Grace being chained to a goddamn wall."

Sam rose from his chair to come around her desk and lean his hip against the edge, right next to Cici's chair, almost but not quite touching her.

"That's a long list."

Cici dropped her face into her hands. "I'm sorry. That's not really fair. None of it."

"So am I." He waited a beat and when he spoke again, his voice was hesitant. "I think I can see where you're coming from. And, yes, I should have trusted you."

Cici dropped her hands and lifted her face to study Sam's. She fumbled but finally managed to grasp his hand.

Sam's gaze dropped to their linked hands. His lids rose slowly and he stared into her eyes for a long moment. The silence grew but, as it did, something softened in his eyes. A hardness that had always been there eased. Finally, Sam squeezed her fingers in gentle thanks.

Before he let go of her hand, Cici raised it and pressed it to her cheek. "I'm scared for Grace. If…if she's not the woman you found today…" She didn't want to admit that it would most likely be Becky Gutierrez's body. "That means she's still trapped."

"I promise I'll take your dreams seriously, Cee. But I have to have evidence. A trail. Something else. Can you tell me where she is?"

"I would if I knew. I wish to God I knew."

"Ah, Cee." Sam slid his fingers into her hair, his thumb rubbing against her temple. His gaze dropped to her lips.

"Kissing you was the biggest mistake," he murmured.

Cici stiffened, hurt and embarrassment slamming through her much as a lance would pierce armor and batter a knight's body. She scooted back, out of his grasp.

"Sam! I was able to get in touch with…" Hannah barreled into Cici's office.

Cici sat back in her chair and gripped the armrests.

"Go on," Sam prodded at Hannah's deer-in-the-headlights expression.

"I-I called my friend—the one who lives in Taos, like you asked. She knows both Grace and Becky."

Sam pulled out the small notebook he always kept in his pocket. "This was Winnie Mendez?"

Hannah nodded.

"Will she talk to me?"

Hannah smiled and handed him a piece of paper. "Yeah, sure. Here's her number. She's waiting for your call."

"Thanks, Hannah. I appreciate you getting on this so quickly."

"No prob." Hannah hesitated at the door, hovering there for another moment. "You okay, Reverend?" she asked.

"I'm fine," Cici replied, straining to keep her voice normal.

"You've been really helpful, Hannah," Sam said. "I appreciate Winnie's number."

Hannah opened her mouth like she wanted to say something more but after a moment, she just turned away. "I'll get back to my knitting group, then."

"Enjoy your afternoon," Cici said.

"Yeah, you, too," Hannah replied.

Sam stared at his notes then tucked the number Hannah gave him carefully into the notebook before he closed it. "I'll call her to set up a time to talk. This has to wait until after I go to Albuquerque." Sam made a frustrated sound. "But first…"

"Don't," Cici said her voice full of censure.

His gaze flashed to hers and she immediately looked away.

"Cici, I didn't mean—"

"Grace needs you to find her."

Sam raised an eyebrow but his eyes hardened. "I need to clarify—"

"Grace said she shouldn't have told him. Then she touched her bruise."

Sam's frustration grew. "Please, Cee. I meant—"

"Henry said she and Becky were looking into their family history. Becky seemed to believe Grace's father's drowning was intentional." She glanced up at him, held his gaze. "That it was murder."

24

Sam

All wickedness comes from weakness. — Rousseau

With a resigned sigh, Sam finally dropped the subject. "Start at the beginning."

Cici wet her lips and began to talk.

When she finished, Sam wanted to tell her she'd make a hell of a detective. That he hadn't meant he didn't want to kiss her, but that he wanted to kiss her too much.

He didn't dare try again. Not right now.

"I'm off." He stood and walked to the door, then turned back, his hand on the jamb. "You want to go to Taos tomorrow?" he asked.

"Me?" Cici asked, startled. "Um…"

"I'd like the company," Sam said, his heart pounding at the thought of her rejecting his overture. "And it's clear Anna Carmen's trying to tell you something. Maybe being closer to where Grace was last…"

"I'll think about it." She sighed.

"I can pick you up in the morning."

"I have a group in at ten. I'll need to lock up here and walk Mona before I can leave."

She didn't want to go with him. Dammit. He'd really messed things up now.

Sam nodded. "That'll give me time to set up my interviews there."

"I'll let you know, okay?"

He patted the jamb. "For the record," Sam dropped his voice and looked up and down the hall to be sure they couldn't be overheard. "I think your first gut instinct about Henry was right. He doesn't have any kind of record with abuse or domestic disturbance. But Esperanza does."

Best he could do right now. Cici's frown told him it wasn't enough.

———

Most of the law enforcement people Sam knew agreed on one thing: the lack of population, thus the lack of facilities was the largest problem with investigating crimes in the state of New Mexico. Yesterday, he'd driven the hour north to Taos; this afternoon, he drove the hour or so south to University of New Mexico's tree-laden campus in the heart of Albuquerque. He turned onto University and followed the pedestrian-filled streets to the OMI building.

Even in summer, students lined the sidewalks and littered the grassy areas, many using their backpacks as pillows as they lazed in the sun.

Sam's father wanted him to go to an Ivy League university—something Sam eschewed mainly to prove he could and would be his own man. Perhaps his father's dire warnings were coming true and Sam would never have a network of well-connected leaders in law and business. Maybe Sam was destined to live in the town he grew up in.

Sam mentally shrugged. New Mexico remained highly under-rated as a place to live—for which Sam was eternally grateful. He enjoyed being back, living here now, much more now since he'd lived in Denver for a while.

He parked in the OMI's lot and headed into the air-conditioned coolness of the building, shivering slightly at the change in temperature. Albuquerque was almost always ten degrees warmer than Santa Fe. The larger city sat nearly two-thousand feet lower than the capital and many of the buildings and homes here required refrigerated air to get through the months of scorching temperatures.

Sam signed in and went through the normal admittance process. He was greeted by Jerrod Wilson, one of the investigators who'd been at the murder scene that morning.

"Let's go on back. We're all set up and ready."

Sam followed, his steps slower. This was not part of the process he enjoyed.

"As you know, she sustained multiple contusions, mainly to the face and neck," Jerrod said. "Blunt trauma. Could be a fist—a large one—but I think it was something else because of the extent of the damage."

Sam pressed his lips together and nodded as they entered the autopsy room. Jerrod pulled back the sheet and Sam inhaled again, shocked by the brutality of the beating.

"I'd almost say a crime of passion except for this," Jerrod said, pointing to the bullet's entry wound.

Two shots, centered together on the chest cavity. Sam bet the person who'd made those had spent some time around weapons, probably even at a shooting range.

"Why did you say that? About a crime of passion? " Sam asked, leaning forward.

"I said it's *not* a crime of passion. She was shot before she was beaten," Jerrod said.

Sam's head came up. "You sure?"

Jerrod nodded.

"The reason to hit her after would be?" Sam asked. But he knew. The sinking in his gut told him that the killer didn't want the woman identified.

———

Sam had stayed while Jerrod measured the wounds and went over the trauma from the bullets and the beating.

"She had asthma," Jerrod said as he examined the lungs. Sam had long since stepped away from the autopsy table, unwilling to remain so close to what had once been a vibrant, living person.

"I'd ask how you know, but I've had enough fun with dead bodies for the day."

Jerrod made a sympathetic sound. "We've been here a couple of hours," he said, glancing up at the clock. "But yes, I'm sure about the asthma."

"So, she probably used an inhaler?"

"That's a good guess."

Sam stood up and came nearer the table. Autopsies were clinical, and they required removal of organs. Right now, the woman looked less like a person and more like…well, like a science experiment. Sam glanced away, hating his train of thought. Cici wouldn't care for it either.

Cici…

"Does she have freckles?" Sam asked, facing Jerrod and the body again. He peered down. Hard to tell under the thick bruising.

The medical examiner began to remove his gloves, but he rolled them back down and bent over the body. "Freckles?"

"On her face, jaw maybe even and neck. I can't see any." Sam said, almost wanting Cici to be wrong. So he could prove Anna Carmen was really gone and ease Cici's concerns over her sister's soul. "Is there some way to tell through the bruising and cuts?"

Jerrod turned her chin, looking at her jaw down to her neck. He pulled out a magnifying glass and studied further. Then, he pointed. "Yes. Here."

Sam closed his eyes briefly. "All right. Check fingerprints and dental against Rebekah Gutierrez."

Jerrod raised his brows but he nodded. He pulled off his gloves and jotted down the note.

"What made you ask about freckles?" he asked.

Sam's guts iced even as his chest eased. "You probably wouldn't believe me."

Jerrod held Sam's gaze. "I've been doing this twenty years. If you have a secret weapon, my suggestion is to keep it close."

For the first time since Sam arrived, he cracked a tiny smile. "I plan on it."

———

Sam made his way back to Santa Fe. He'd called ahead, so Yolanda would still be waiting at the CYFD child services division on Fifth

Street. He exited Saint Francis and headed north toward Saint Michael's Drive, where he cursed the engineer who'd created the terrible honeycomb exit from the main north/south thoroughfare onto one of the most-trafficked east/west roads.

He glanced at the Kmart as he turned onto Fifth. Used to be a vibrant store—hell, the whole area had once been vibrant, but the decline of the Kmart and the Walmart just down Cerrillos settled this area of town into…not disrepair or even disrepute, but it wasn't as clean or prosperous as it had been during his youth.

A quick right turn and he parked in the CYFD child service lot. The front door allowed for a left or right—Sam turned toward the CS portion, thankful he wasn't dealing with a juvenile justice case. Those were always depressing.

He signed in at the front desk and settled into one of the narrow chairs to wait. His contact for the case, Yolanda, called him back a few minutes later. She was a forty-something no-nonsense woman with dark hair and thick, chunky glasses. Sam liked her efficiency.

"We placed the child. A nice single woman. She takes in a lot of our younger emergencies. A former school teacher. Good home, great record."

"You sure?" Sam asked. At Yolanda's souring look, he said, "I promised Cici—sorry, Reverend Gurule—I would confirm."

Yolanda fiddled with her pen. "I know her. She helps out at the shelters, with the kids. You tell her best as I can tell, yes."

"No problems? With the baby?"

Yolanda's gaze turned sharp. "No. None. Should I be worried?"

Sam swallowed. "You're Becky Gutierrez's direct supervisor,

right?"

Yolanda nodded.

"Has she called in? Touched base with anyone here?"

Yolanda's frown deepened. "No. But she's off this week."

"When we spoke yesterday, you said this time off was a sudden decision. When did she ask for the vacation days?"

"Last Thursday evening. She left me a message." Yolanda tapped the phone. "I was kind of surprised, to be honest. Becky's never done anything like that before. But she said there was a family emergency and she needed the time."

"Do you know where she was? What the emergency was?"

"No." Yolanda cleared her throat, clearly not liking Sam's line of questioning. "She didn't say."

Sam pulled out his notebook and fiddled with it, searching for a clean page. "Do you know what Becky did for fun? Who she hung out with?"

Yolanda considered before shaking her head. "You'd have to ask her coworkers for more information."

Sam planned on it.

"But I do know she spent time with her cousin," Yolanda said. "Becky said Grace was her only family in town."

"And did the women do anything together? Did Becky talk about their activities?"

"Well…" Yolanda settled her chin on her open palm. "She mentioned a project they were working on." Yolanda pursed her lips. "I only heard it in a passing remark. Something about their family. I assumed that meant genealogy."

Sam finished writing down Yolanda's comments and closed his

book. "You've been really helpful. Mind if I speak with the staff?"

Yolanda stood and shook his hand. "Please. Those who are still here, anyway. Do you…why are you asking about Becky?" Her voice quavered as if she, too, already understood the situation.

"I don't have anything confirmed," Sam said.

Yolanda's hand fluttered to her chest. "But?"

Sam shook his head. "We haven't been able to get in touch with her."

"Does this have something to do with one of her cases?" Yolanda scrunched her eyes closed. "We let those women, social workers, without the proper police-style training you have, walk into apartments with the worst of people…" Yolanda looked up, her eyes glassy. "They go by themselves."

Sam nodded. He knew this. One of the worst parts about being a government agency was lack of funding. Social workers went to homes without another person or police backup—into situations that, at times, scared Sam.

"I'll keep you posted. Keep Isabel Bruin safe, okay?"

Yolanda nodded, her eyes dark with worry. "This has something to do with her family. The MMW or whatever."

Sam tilted his head. MMW. That reminded him of something. "Why do you say that?"

"Because last Monday she came into the office all abuzz. She was super excited. Becky didn't do excited. She said they'd found evidence."

"Of what?" Sam asked.

Yolanda shook her head. "I don't know. But I sure wish I'd asked."

25

Sam

Patience is bitter, but its fruit is sweet. — *Rousseau*

Sam called back up to Taos and spoke with all three of his counterparts, putting them on speakerphone.

"It seems our missing women were looking into the murders of Grace's grandmother and aunt. Becky believed Grace's father was murdered, too."

"Oh, please," Phil grumbled. "John and I worked that case together. He just didn't want to marry Esperanza Ahtone." He paused. "Or maybe Fred didn't want him to."

"That your take on it, John?" Sam asked.

The Skype line crackled. "He drowned in the lake. Middle of summer. No witnesses."

So John had doubts. Phil snorted again. "You left out the empty six-pack in his car."

"All right. Let's focus on what we know and what we can dig out," Kent said. The younger man's initiative surprised Sam. "I'll go talk to Fred Ahtone again."

"I'd like to speak with him, too," Sam said. "After I talk to my other folks."

"Then you better hurry back up here," Kent said.

"You know any places with basements up your way?" Sam asked.

"Sure. We got some hunting cabins, some of the bigger houses that have 'em," Phil said. "Why?"

"I have a potential lead on Grace Bruin. We think she's being held in a basement."

"Really?" John asked. "That's great! Any idea what part of town or county to start in?"

"No," Sam admitted.

"I'll compile a list in the county," John said. "Kent, handle the Pueblo and Phil, you get your list of city structures with basements."

"Yeah, I'm on it," Phil grumbled. He clicked off, followed by Kent.

John held the line for another moment. "I have those case files you mentioned," he said to Sam. "Fred's wife, sister, and Esperanza's boyfriend. I worked on two of them. We'll look them over tomorrow."

Sam agreed and hung up, unsure what else to say. But it was clear John and Phil did not agree on much.

Sam woke early the next morning to a confirmation message from Jerrod, sent late the night before: the body from the alley matched Becky Gutierrez's fingerprints and dental records.

He went for a long run, not stopping until his sides heaved and his body dripped with sweat. After a shower and an English muffin he slathered in almond butter—along with at least three cups of coffee—Sam headed to the crime scene.

The note pinned to Becky's blouse, specifically, was bothering him. *Who* was next? He refused to allow Cici to die, but if Becky was dead…then it became more likely the killer meant Grace.

Who was still missing and quite possibly being held hostage in the basement of a cabin. At least Sam had help there, narrowing down the possible residences he'd need to visit.

Sam walked the center of the alley, each time moving out two feet. He wasn't sure when or why he'd come up with this method, but it had worked in the past and was now an ingrained part of his routine.

The body itself offered little: the note pinned to her blouse, the pacifier from the pocket. No car keys. No wallet, purse, anything. If she had asthma, she would have carried an inhaler.

He'd left a message last night with Becky's doctor, but that was after hours. It was still too early to try the office again. Instead, Sam focused on the crime scene. He stepped out again, almost hitting the walls of the building. One last slow, methodical lap.

He reached the large trash receptacle, which his team had emptied in hopes of finding something related to the victim. So far, no luck. Sam crouched down and shone his flashlight under and behind the large metal bin. Nothing.

He stood, dusted his knees and turned. A hunched figure shuffled across the mouth of the alley. Sam followed.

"May I talk to you?" Sam asked. He pulled out his identification and introduced himself, as he did each time he approached one of the vagrants. Yes, this, too was Cici's influence; she'd reminded Sam that just because people lived on the streets did not mean they lost their ability to feel.

The man had graying hair and dark skin that sagged around his eyes and mouth from dissipation and hard street living. Santa Fe didn't have a huge homeless population, but this guy was a regular and known to be helpful, especially to Sam. He knew Cici from one of the shelters and she sometimes dragged Sam to volunteer.

The entire homeless population became more eager to help him after that.

"Gary, isn't it?"

Gary nodded, wary.

"There was a woman killed there the other night," Sam said, thrusting his thumb back toward the alley.

Gary glanced back at it, then up at Sam. "I don't want no trouble. No trouble."

Sam's chest tightened. "Why do you say that, Gary? Did you happen to see something? Something that could identify her or the person who…"

"She was wheezing," Gary mumbled. "I didn't like that sound. Like…like that whooping cough people got a few years back. But the man who held her told her to shut up. She didn't have no medicine. She needed it."

"You sure it was a man?" Sam asked. He pulled out his notebook and jotted down the details.

"I'm sure. Big guy. He had gray in his hair. Collar pulled up on his coat. Wore nice shoes. Like yours."

"Did you see anything else?" Sam asked.

Gary shook his head. "I don't want to go to the station. Officer Rawley don't like me."

Sam patted Gary's shoulder. "All right. But if you think of anything, will you get in touch with me?"

Gary wouldn't, but Sam needed to ask and might very well need to bring him in for questioning about the murder. Gary began shuffling down the street again, his many pairs of pants and thin but oversize coat giving his average frame a bulkier appearance. He flicked his fingers in a come-on gesture. Sam followed.

The vagrant headed along East San Francisco, past the Plaza. He shuffled along Cathedral Place but kept on past the Cathedral of Saint Francis toward the parking lot. A lone trash bin sat in the dusty ground between the lot and the lush grounds of the Cathedral.

Gary rested his hand on the chipped metal bin. "People throw away all kinds of stuff down here. What with all the tourists." He met Sam's eyes, his a bit rheumy. "That girl didn't deserve what that man done to her."

Sam nodded his understanding as Gary turned and strolled back toward the Plaza. Sam pulled out his phone and requested assistance to collect the trash bags from all the cans up and down this street, to and from the Plaza.

A smart felon would separate Becky's belongings, which would string out the time it would take for the police to piece together enough of a picture of Becky's activities that evening.

But Sam was putting together the puzzle, even with what little he had to go on: he had impounded Grace's car that had been parked in the lot nearby. The car held a car seat. Becky had a pacifier in her pocket.

Becky must have brought baby Isabel to Cici, just as Cici

had dreamed. If Becky worried about the police in Taos, then dropping the baby on Cici's doorstep practically guaranteed Sam's involvement. Sam had worked with Becky a couple of times. She was knowledgeable about the law and protective services but she was also street smart—Yolanda said Becky was the only Child Services employee to note the gun and the drugs in the test apartment CYFD set up before allowing their new employees to go into homes.

But why would she come to the Plaza? Her apartment was off St. Michael's Drive, a good ten minutes south. Unless…unless she wanted to be surrounded by people. Perhaps she thought she was followed? Either all the way from Taos or from Cici's house, at least.

The Plaza area was always the busiest part of the city with lots of shops, hotels, and restaurants. Maybe Becky planned to lose herself in the crowds.

Yeah, she must have been followed. She might have even tried to go home first, before returning to the Plaza and its crowds. Unfortunately for Becky, she was discovered somewhere along the way and murdered—all within hours of dropping Isabel off at Cici's.

Which brought Sam back around to the MMW Yolanda had heard Becky mention.

MMW. Sam pulled out his phone and looked up the acronym. He shook his head at the Google hits: Making Me Write, Makes Me Want to Die. No, those couldn't be correct. A hip-hop group. Making of the Modern World—some division at a university.

Yolanda must not have gotten the acronym right. No one else he'd spoken with at CYFD last evening had mentioned those letters or remembered Becky talking about it. Could be Yolanda misheard a conversation. Faced with that dead end, Sam went back to the trash cans, continuing his search through the items in them.

By the time Kevin, Damian, and the department's newest detective showed up, Sam had found a small silver purse. In it was a set of keys. One had a Honda logo, reinforcing Sam's belief that Becky took Grace's car with the purpose of driving Isabel to Cici's house.

No wallet or phone, both of which Sam wanted. They might be in another trash can in the vicinity. Sam grabbed a pair of gloves from Kevin and pulled out an important item: the gray inhaler with Rebekah Gutierrez's name on it.

Handwritten on the back in the same bubbly writing were the numbers: 705. Beneath that, part of letters were visible CIV.

If that was Becky's final message, he didn't understand the code.

26

Cici

What good would it be to possess the whole universe
if one were its only survivor? — Rousseau

The house was quiet—too quiet. Cici worried the edge of the blanket that lay over her lap as she stared at a rerun of *I Love Lucy.*

Cici feared to fall asleep nearly as much as she hoped she'd get more information. Eventually, her eyes slid shut, and a new vision gripped her.

Grace stood in a damp, dark room. Her clothes smelled of body odor and mildew. Her hair fell in thick tangles around her cheeks.

She hurt everywhere, especially her wrists, which were wrapped with handcuffs and chained to the wall.

Her arm ached and her left eye throbbed, the swelling so great she could no longer see out of it. Her lip split and blood dribbled down her chin.

Grace wiped it with her unchained hand. A smear of red stained her skin next to her large diamond engagement ring and a narrower gold band.

"This is all your fault!"

The savage voice, like the blow that followed it, shocked Grace so much, she fell onto her knees and slammed against the wall. Small, sharp rocks dug into her knees. As she braced herself, preparing to stand, pain splintered through her middle. She rolled over, gasping against what must be broken ribs, to look up into a mottled, enraged face.

When the man raised his leg again, Grace moaned.

"No, please. Stop."

She rolled away even as the man kicked again. Grace's heart slammed inside her chest. Was she...

"Your fault, Grace," the man growled. His breath slipped past his lips in a deep, harsh pant that reached her, causing her to want to curl up tighter.

Her breath caught. Holy hell, she hurt. If this is what Sam went through as a child, no wonder he hated to discuss it—to ever relive even a moment of his life with such a monster.

"He told you to stop searching."

Grandfather had told Grace many things, but never that monsters like this one existed.

The man stepped into a narrow beam of light, which turned his eyes nearly translucent and limned his hair in a halo he did not deserve.

"Did you listen?"

Clearly a rhetorical question.

"I'll find her," he spat.

"Becky will tell," Grace mumbled in a quavering voice.

"No, she won't. She won't have time."

He stormed up the short flight of stairs that left from the cellar, a thick, wooden storm door slamming shut behind him.

He would hurt Henry, too, as he'd threatened before.

Thank God Grace sent the message to Becky, letting her know where to look.

Becky took Isabel—she'd be fine. She'd be safe with Reverend Gurule. The reverend's detective friend would make sure of it.

His tires crunched over the gravel in the drive. Some of the rocks thumped against the wooden door. Grace sagged against the wall, tipping her head back.

Becky would be okay, too. She had a fifteen, maybe even twenty-minute head start. No way he could get to Becky in time.

No way.

Sirens turned on, screaming out in the night.

She sagged against the bonds and let the tears fall.

None of them was safe. He was the police.

———

Cici called and texted Sam but didn't hear back. She hoped he'd get to her as soon as he could. The day slid past in a blur of too much to do. Carina, hair curled and wearing a cute sundress, stopped by.

"Mom's with Laurel for the next couple hours, and I needed to get out of the house. We're going to lunch."

Cici hugged her friend and smiled. "I wish I could, but I'm slammed. And I'm waiting to talk to Sam."

"You need an assistant, girlfriend. And Sam can wait on you for a change." At Cici's look, she waggled her finger and said, "You know I'm right, and you're killing yourself. That was never the plan. Come on, let's talk about it over lunch. Board of directors' orders."

———

"Do you have anyone in mind?" Carina asked as Cici settled her napkin in her lap.

They sat on the patio of Restaurant Martin, one of Carina's favorite eateries. The chef had already greeted her and asked about her young daughter.

"Not really, no," Cici said. "But I do have a question. Well, more of a favor."

"Shoot," Carina said, lifting her delicate crystal glass filled with water.

"As a mom of a baby, what would make you disappear?"

Carina set the glass down on the table. "What do you mean?"

"From your daughter's life? Is there anything that would make you leave her?"

Carina shook her head, adamant. "No. Nothing."

"Not if Jacob hit you?"

Carina shook her head again. "There's nothing, Cici. Not one thing. If—and that's totally hypothetical because if Jacob hit me, I'd leave his sorry ass and take all his money—if he hit me, I'd grab Laurel and we'd leave together."

"That's what's bothering me about Sam's current case." She explained an abbreviated storyline for Carina, who hung on her every word.

"She went to her," Carina said.

"What?"

"The mom. Grace. She went to her baby. That's the only reason she would walk out without a word. To protect her daughter."

"You think so?" Cici asked, and at Carina's nod, continued, "I do, too."

The waiter set their large platters of salad and fresh fish on the table. Cici inhaled the delicious, spicy smells as her stomach grumbled. She couldn't remember her last decent meal. Carina was right, she needed an assistant.

"I know so. Look, Cici. When you have a kid…" Carina paused. "When you have a baby that you wanted, when you love that child, you'd do anything—I mean anything—to keep your baby safe. That's why there's that saying about your heart being outside your body."

Cici wasn't familiar with the saying, but she understood the gist of what Carina was telling her.

"What about a father?" Cici asked, thinking about Henry.

Carina chewed a bite of food, her eyes never leaving Cici's. "Jacob would commit crimes for our girl, Cee."

Cici nodded before she stared down at her plate, her appetite vanquished by worry.

Sam popped his head around Cici's door just after she'd gotten on a phone call. She waved, then held up her finger.

Mrs. Sanchez answered on the third ring. The older woman was a dame of Santa Fe—her family tree's roots dated back to before the Pueblo Rebellion.

Cici explained her problem, ignoring Sam's raised eyebrows.

"*No hay problema, Reverenda*," Mrs. Sanchez said. "You saved my son and grandson. I'll just be your new secretary. I need something to do with my day now that Miguel and Juan moved out for good. And the daytime TV—don't get me started."

"You know I'd love you to work with me, Mrs. Sanchez, but there's a hiring process—"

Sam smirked as he dropped into the club chair across from her desk.

"I'll talk to the deacons and get my forms filled out. I'm not working on Friday afternoon or Saturdays, though. I have my bunco and gardening clubs."

"Um…"

"I heard you're helping your detective friend with another case. You just go on and get that nice boy Henry his baby home. You better help him get the baby back, Reverend," Mrs. Sanchez said, steamrolling over Cici's wilting protests. "Or I'm going to quit working for you and suggest we all go back to Santo de Niño."

That was a large Catholic church on the south side of town. "I'll do my best, Mrs. Sanchez, but this is more Sam's wheel-house. I just needed to make sure everyone could get into the church when they needed to—"

The line clicked off and Cici stared at her now-black phone screen, her stomach aching from lack of food and concern over what havoc she'd managed to create both for her churchgoers and herself with one phone call.

"Call went well?" Sam asked.

He handed Cici a large coffee. She took a sip and closed her eyes as the heat slid down her throat.

"I think I just hired Mrs. Sanchez as the church secretary," Cici said

"Huh." Sam took a long drink of his coffee, probably so he

didn't have to say anything else. Cici understood his reticence. Mrs. Sanchez was a force—one of those strong-willed women who accomplished what she set out to do.

"I'm heading up to Taos now. Got caught up in some stuff here earlier. Have you talked to Henry?"

Cici shook her head.

"I did, earlier. I wanted you to know I messed up." Sam's face contorted into a pained expression. "Because of what happened to me, I kind of expected that to be the situation with the Bruins."

Cici waited.

"And it's not," Sam said on a sigh.

Cici leaned forward and laid her palm over his forearm. Sam surprised her by taking her hand in his. They sat like that for a long moment.

"I had another dream. Last night," Cici said, her voice quiet. She really didn't want to relive that one. But Sam needed to know.

He set his coffee on Cici's desk and untangled their fingers to pull out his notebook and pen.

"Did you…ah…can you come up to Taos with me?" Sam asked, his voice hesitant.

Cici shook her head, trying to ignore Sam's disappointment. "I'm here by myself today and one of the toilets overflowed. I'm waiting on the plumber."

Sam nodded, looking mollified by her response. But even if she didn't have to stay at the church, Cici still wouldn't have gone to Taos with him. She was too confused by his hot-and-cold responses to her. She needed time and space to sort through her jumbled emotions.

"What are we going to do about Henry?" Cici asked.

Sam slid his hands into his slacks pockets and pushed out his legs as he leaned back in the chair. "Well, I'm going to go to his hearing and explain that I jumped the gun on this one. It's scheduled for tomorrow at ten."

Cici startled. "I didn't know that. I'll go, too."

"Tell me about your dream," Sam said.

She did. With each word, Sam's expression turned more grim.

"The deceased was identified," Sam said. "It's Becky Gutierrez. And, after this, I don't think we'll find Esperanza alive."

"That's not your biggest problem," Cici said. She took a deep breath. "The murderer? It's definitely a cop."

27

Sam

*I would rather be a man of paradoxes than a man
of prejudices. —Rousseau*

Sam called ahead as he drove north back toward Taos, talking
to Kent, Phil, and John separately this time. Kent promised to
run by Fred's place whereas John was a step ahead and, after not
receiving an answer after his last stop-in the night before, had
asked the judge for a search warrant for Esperanza Ahtone's place.

Sam clicked on his blinker and turned onto one of the side
streets. He turned again into a neat neighborhood with small
stucco-clad homes and checked his GPS before rolling to a stop
in front of one, eschewing the short driveway.

Phil exited his car and met him at the walk.

"Any word on Esperanza or Grace?" Sam asked.

"That's John's territory," Phil said with a shrug.

They headed up the narrow flagstone path. The air was a few
degrees cooler—with less energy-zapping bite—than in Santa Fe.
Sam inhaled the clean, mountain air with relish.

"I had some people check out a few of the houses here with
basements. You know, the ones with known criminals. We got
nothing," Phil said.

Sam nodded, unsurprised. Right now, he was searching for the proverbial needle in a haystack.

A few weeds and other plants shot up between the stones, but like the flowerbeds, the yard had a well-kept charm.

A woman answered the door after Sam rang the bell. He squinted, trying to get a better idea of the woman's age through the screen.

"Winnie?" Sam asked.

"Yes."

Sam pulled out his badge and ID, showing her both. "I'm Detective Samuel Chastain with the Santa Fe Police Department and this is Detective Phil Hartman of the Taos Police Department. I spoke with you on the phone yesterday."

Winnie pushed open the screen door. "Yes, of course. Come on in."

They walked straight into a small living room. The Saltillo tiles were covered in black-and-white wool rugs each in a different Native American design.

"I love your rugs," Phil said, bending closer to examine them. "My ex-wife was nuts for the local weavers. We had a few that were made in Chimayó."

Winnie frowned. "I keep thinking I should take them up off the floor because they're worth a lot, but my father bought them for my mother, like, thirty-five years ago as an anniversary gift. My mom refuses, saying this is what they're meant for."

Phil chuckled. "I wouldn't know. Lost them in the divorce."

"I appreciate your willingness to meet with us," Sam said, stepping into the ensuing silence. "I know you spoke with

Hannah Ross earlier. She's a friend of yours?"

Winnie nodded. "We did our undergrad degrees together at UNM."

"I'm a Lobo, too," Sam said. "Graduated nine years ago. Our football team is still crap."

Winnie laughed. "So, Hannah said you had some questions about Grace Bruin and her cousin Becky."

"We do, yes," Sam said. "I'd like to jump right in. When was the last time you saw them?"

Winnie pulled out one of those old-school paper planners and a pair of reading glasses. "I write everything down. I'm too worried about losing my phone or having the operating system crash." She shrugged. "I'm sure that makes me seem neurotic, but it works for me."

She flipped to a page she'd marked with a narrow pink sticky note. "I saw Beck and Grace the day Grace's daughter went missing. That was terrible." Winnie's face contorted in a grimace.

She slid her glasses off and nibbled at one of the ends. As if noticing her bad habit, she plunked her glasses on top of her head.

"I asked Beck what was going on."

"What did she say?" Phil asked.

"That Isabel's abduction was payback."

Sam made a careful note in his notebook, frowning. "For what?"

Winnie shrugged. "I don't know."

"Henry said Grace came up to Taos about once a week to see you. What did you ladies do?"

Winnie's face scrunched in confusion. "Before her daughter disappeared, I hadn't seen Grace in…" Her gaze drifted off as she fell into thought. "I hadn't seen Grace in probably three months."

"She never stopped by?" Sam asked.

Winnie scrunched up her brows, considering. "I saw her one time." Winnie flipped through her planner. "That was my night to cook dinner here, and I'd blanked on it," she mumbled, her brow deeply furrowed. "I went to the store," she explained. "Grace was there, picking up some groceries. She said they were for her grandfather, but I didn't think the two of them got along. I mean, no one really got along with Mr. Ahtone."

"Why not?" Phil asked.

"He's just…well, he's mean." Winnie looked down, obviously embarrassed.

"How was she, Grace, that day you saw her? How did she act?"

"She acted weird," Winnie said. "She had a bruise on her cheek. Well, not a bruise. More of a pink spot. Like she'd been hit."

"Did Grace say anything about that?" Sam asked.

"No, I pretended not to notice."

Sam clicked his pen a few times

"How about bruises or broken bones?" Phil persisted. "Wrapped up joints or long-sleeves in the summer?"

"Not since Grace left the Pueblo." Winnie pulled her glasses off her head and fiddled with them. "I—I think her mom used to hit her."

Winnie whispered this. Sam tensed but made an effort to keep his outward appearance calm.

"Why's that?" Sam asked, his voice gentle.

"Becky told me so," Winnie mumbled the words together quickly.

"When?" Sam asked.

"When Isabel disappeared. She said Grace's idea to find out what happened to her grandma was stupid because it wouldn't make Esperanza love Grace now."

"Is that what she was doing?" Sam asked. "Up here? Looking into her grandmother's murder?"

Winnie shook her head. "I guess. I didn't really understand. They kept talking about something called MMIW."

28

Sam

The real world has its limits; the imaginary world is infinite.
Unable to enlarge the one, let us restrict the other, for it is
from the difference between the two alone that are born all
the pains which make us truly unhappy. — Rousseau

Those initials again. Well, this time with the I. Sam pulled out his phone to look it up. Right then Phil stalked out of the house, knocking into his arm, causing Sam to drop his phone. Picking it back up, he was annoyed both with Phil and with the new dent in his case. At least the screen hadn't cracked.

"What a goddamn waste of time," Phil muttered.

"You think so?" Sam asked.

"What did we learn? Grace had family issues. She wanted to solve her grandmother's death to earn love. Someone—more than likely her husband hit her. Good thing you got that baby into foster. You did, right?"

"We're working on it," Sam said.

Kent pulled up in his battered old truck. He rolled down the window and leaned out. "Hey, detectives. Did you already talk to Winnie?"

"Sure did," Sam said. He powered on his phone, planning to

look up those initials again.

"Oh. Well. John wants you to come out to Esperanza's place."

"Why's that?" Phil asked, still obviously annoyed.

"We found Esperanza."

Sam's stomach tightened painfully as he slid his phone into his pocket. "Alive?"

Kent shook his head.

"All right," Sam said. He scrubbed his hand over his head. "We'll follow you."

———

Sam was the last car in the procession until John Milstead's cruiser pulled in behind his. The four vehicles made the slow progress up the steep hillside. They stopped in front of the small adobe-and-wood structure settled in the middle of a sparse pine forest. A deep ravine slashed the landscape to the west and the mountain rose, majestic to the north.

The men exited their cars, and Sam fell into step beside John. The terrain was jagged as they neared the ravine. Sam stopped and crouched. He gestured to John.

"Is that…"

"Looks like," John said, his voice turning as grim as the set of his lips. "He must've beat her good before she fell in the ravine."

"Or was pushed," Sam said as he rose, his gaze sweeping the area. He glanced back at Kent and Phil before following the trail of small, almost imperceptible drips to the edge of the ravine.

The shattered body lay, bent at awkward angles, at the bottom. She'd been there a while—her pecked-at flesh and tattered clothing that spoke of days, not mere hours.

Sam should have insisted on a search warrant days before. He just hadn't had enough evidence then.

"Been dead long enough for both the coyotes and the birds to get to her," John said, voicing Sam's frustrations. He shook his head, eyes dark with concern. "Damn," he muttered in a quiet voice.

Kent shuffled closer, hands stuffed into his pockets. "It's not looking good for Grace Bruin," he said on a sigh.

"Nope," Sam said.

"Places like these, it's always the indigenous women," Kent said.

Sam's stomach tingled. Indigenous women. There'd been a big social media push about that after Standing Rock. Something to do with the MeToo movement.

Kent made a gesture and hummed something that Sam guessed must be Hopi. Maybe a prayer for the dead. Sam planned to ask, but Kent bowed his head.

"This is why I got into this work. For the Missing and Murdered Indigenous Women. Like my sister," Kent said on a long sigh.

29

Sam

To be sane in a world of madman is in itself madness. — Rousseau

"MMIW—that's the acronym," Sam exclaimed.

"What?" Kent asked, turning toward him. His expression was still pained, but his gaze was intent, almost hawklike as he focused on Sam.

"MMIW. MMW. Yolanda was close. Becky," Sam began to explain. "In her note that she left with Isabel. She said they shouldn't have looked into the deaths. And Yolanda, Becky's boss, said Becky had been talking about MMW—she'd gotten it wrong. Winnie mentioned it, too. MMIW. Missing and Murdered Indigenous Women."

"All right. I'm following you," Kent said.

"Well, if Becky and Grace were looking into…what did John say? Grace's grandmother was killed?"

Kent nodded. He waved John over. "Listen to this," he said, motioning Sam to continue.

"Grace's grandmother was murdered."

John nodded. "So was her great aunt. Has to be close to forty years ago now."

"The murders," Sam said. He realized he'd never shown the men the note. He didn't have email access all the way out there. "It's in Becky's note. The one she left with the baby."

"That would have helped us earlier," John said, his tone dry.

Sam raised an eyebrow. "So would have knowing so many women in Grace and Becky's family were murdered before last night."

John rocked back on his heels. "Point."

"So, we know Becky and Grace were looking into their deaths, probably because of the MMIW social media movement," Kent said.

"What are you talking about?" Phil asked, joining them.

"I think I've found the connection," Sam said.

"Oh?" Phil asked. "What's that?"

"We have a killer who's gone after Tiwa women, indigenous women. Possibly for decades," Sam said.

Kent studied the three men. "If we have a local murderer, how do we know he's still active?"

"And what about the baby? Why take her?" John asked.

Sam shook his head. "I don't know. But I want to talk to Cici…"

"Who?" Kent asked.

"My friend," Sam said. "She had a dream. Before we found Becky." He chose not to say anything about the waking one Cici had yesterday, not wanting to undermine her credibility.

"I'll call her once we get off the mountain. See if she's picked up anything else."

"That's strong medicine," John said. "If she has the sight, I mean."

"You have family in the Pueblo?" Sam asked.

"This one?" John asked. "No. I'm part Navajo. Mom's side."

"Like me," Kent said. "Not many have the sight. At least that I have heard of. Is your friend from one of the Pueblos?"

Sam shook his head.

John and Kent deflated. "You should still talk to her," John said.

"I need to go back to Becky Gutierrez's family home. I'd planned to talk to her mother, Gemma, before Kent let us know you'd found Esperanza's body."

"I already sent out a patrol," Phil said. "You know, to let the family know about Becky's death. They're not going to be ready to talk to you yet."

Sam swallowed down his irritation. He glanced at John, who stood, arms crossed, staring at the trail of cars coming up the narrow, rutted track toward Esperanza's house. No wonder John disliked working with Phil. The man kept getting in the way of Sam's investigation.

"Fine," Sam said on a sigh. "What about Fred Ahtone?" he asked Kent.

"Talked to the old man before I came into town. He's not saying anything."

"I guess I'll head back to Santa Fe, then. One of my guys found Becky's wallet and phone in our trash search. He called while I was driving up to let me know it was going to the lab guys. I want to know what's on that, STAT."

John continued to stand at the edge of the ravine, legs spread.

"I'll manage this here," he said. "And let's be in touch soon."

Sam nodded as he, Kent, and Phil walked toward their cars. Shame washed over Sam as he realized he'd dismissed Cici's early attempts to explain the continued identical twin telepathy. Mainly because he didn't want Cici to believe everything Anna Carmen could tell her…about him.

In doing so, Sam hurt Cici. Made her question her ability to cope with grief and possibly her sanity. Now, however, he needed to use her connection to help him solve the case.

Yeah, he was a total ass.

Sam climbed into his police vehicle. He headed off the mountain and called his boss to let him know the current state of the investigation. He'd call Cici once he made it back to the main highway—the reception up here was terrible.

His radio crackled and Sam cursed when he heard there was an accident on 285—the main road between Santa Fe and Taos.

Sam pulled onto one of the smaller, windy roads that cut off about fifteen miles from his trip back to Santa Fe. The sooner he got back, the sooner he could go through Becky's texts and messages. Sam hoped he'd get a better idea of who their suspect was from Becky's phone because the information on the inhaler didn't tell him enough.

The road hair-pinned down the side of the mountain, but it was rarely crowded, making it his best option.

Sam finished pulling out of an S-curve, frowning as he caught sight of a vehicle barreling close behind him.

It slammed into him, hard.

Sam struggled to maintain control of his car, but he lost it when the other vehicle slammed into him, harder, a second time, edging into the passenger side of the small sedan.

Sam yelled, his voice filled with defiance and fear. The third collision sent his car careening over the side of the narrow road, straight down the side of the mountain.

Sam hated roller coasters because of the push of gravity, the sensation of falling. This misadventure created about a thousand times more G-force, more falling and a much, much harder landing.

Sam catapulted forward, his knee slamming into the steering wheel a second before the airbag there deployed, filling his nose with a gross white powder.

A terrible shriek rent the air as the vehicle continued to slide downward, farther off the road over the rocks and gravel strewn between juniper. The car finally ground to a halt with a soft jerk.

The airbag deflated in a slow hiss. Sam groaned out a few choice curses. He glanced down at his torso now sprinkled in shards of windshield glass. He shook his head, trying to keep his mind clear and focused. Shock. He was in shock.

He wiggled his fingers and toes, then his arms. He dipped his head back and forth on his neck, wincing slightly when the muscles caught. He moved to his legs and bit back another curse. Yep, his knee was already swollen.

He placed his hand on his thigh, wrapping his fingers around his kneecap as he winced. He hoped none of the ligaments were torn.

"Call for help," Sam muttered, pulling out his phone.

No service. Of course.

What did he know about the situation? He spoke aloud, into his phone's recording app. "A dark SUV. I think it was a Jeep. Not a new one. I caught a B and an X off the license plate from my rearview mirror before I went over the side."

He managed to unclip his safety belt.

"Three hits is the charm," Sam said, his tone drier than a June afternoon. "No sirens. No help forthcoming. So, definitely intentional."

He turned off his phone and shoved it into his slacks pocket. Sam pulled his pistol from its holster and opened his door. He grunted to get it all the way open, working against gravity.

With one arm used in an armbar, Sam moved his way out of the vehicle, eyes darting as he surveyed the area. Sam winced when he put his full weight on his swollen knee. He walked around the perimeter of the crash area.

Nothing.

At least he was alone. He glanced up. A few hundred feet, pretty much straight up. He looked down. The ground was more level, easier to traverse. Gritting his teeth, Sam began the long, hard trek down the mountain toward the main highway.

He had maybe another hour of daylight, but thereafter, temperatures would drop—probably close to freezing since he was over eight thousand feet—the deeper into the night he had to walk.

Best chance at quick discovery was to hail a passing car, which meant getting to the highway as quickly as possible.

Twilight came and went. Sam holstered his weapon. As the darkness deepened, Sam began to shiver as the sweat from his exertions cooled over his exposed skin. The faint hum of road noise drifted up the mountainside, but he was still too far away to flag down a car. Sam pulled out his phone and frowned at the screen.

Still no signal. With a sigh, he shoved the phone back into his pocket.

He worked his way around a big, gray striated boulder, speeding up as the car sounds grew louder.

That sudden burst of speed probably saved his life. Because a moment later, the sound of a shotgun being cocked caused Sam to stumble.

30

Cici

He who blushes is already guilty. — *Rousseau*

Cici glanced over at the large-faced iron-and-wood clock that hung from a wooden peg in her living room—it was one of Cici's favorite pieces. She'd found it at one of the many consignment shops in town and splurged, calling it an early birthday present—or, maybe better, a she-survived-certain-death present.

It was after eleven at night.

Sam hadn't called. He'd said he'd check in. She'd texted him a few times now and it was unlike him to forget.

She walked back into the kitchen and collected the extra set of keys to Sam's house. She headed to her laundry room and grabbed the dogs' leashes. She clicked them on and settled the dogs into the car.

She'd wait at Sam's house for him to return.

———

Cici woke, her body shaking from the dream. She lay there, shuddering in the dark. She was pretty sure he was hurt. Something about a winding road and a Jeep.

"Sam," she gasped.

She glanced at her clock. Just after two in the morning. She covered her eyes with her arm and moaned.

She picked up her phone. Still nothing from him.

"Dammit, Aci. This is too much."

She dialed the front dispatch for the police department.

"Santa Fe Police Department."

"Hi. This is Reverend Cecilia Gurule. I'm trying to reach Detective Sam Chastain. Is he in the precinct, by chance?"

"No, Reverend. I haven't seen him since I came on shift at ten."

Cici worried her lip. "Do you know when he last checked in?"

"I'm sorry, I don't. Want me to leave a note for Jen?"

"Yes, please. I…" Cici swallowed down her next words: I have a really bad feeling. "Thanks."

"No problem. Have a good night."

Cici hung up. She sat her phone on Sam's scuffed coffee table and considered her choices.

She was past worried. The dream spooked her. She tried his number again.

Straight to voicemail.

She'd come to his place because she needed to apologize—as he had to her yesterday. She'd been upset with the situation more so than with Sam himself, and she really shouldn't be angry with him for doing his job. But now…now she feared Sam was in danger and she didn't know where he was or how to help.

She huddled on his couch, clutching her phone, saying prayer after prayer.

She never even realized she'd fallen back asleep.

She just was…there, in that dank pit once again. Waiting. Hurting.

———

Grace gasped as light flooded the space. She braced herself for him. For the blows.

"Oh, my darling," Esperanza gasped.

She moved down the steps, heedless of how fast she flew.

"No, Mom. You can't be here."

Esperanza lifted her daughter's face and studied the bruised mass. "I've been wrong. About so many things."

"Go," Grace whispered. "Go. He'll come back soon."

"He won't hurt you again," Esperanza promised. "I should never have hit you, baby. I'm so sorry." Tears spilled from her eyes as she shoved a bobby pin into the lock. She tucked her tongue in the corner of her lip and twisted, her face contorting as she tried to pry open the lock.

"Go, Mom. Get help. Call…" Grace's breath failed her.

The woman rose, unsteadily to her feet. She lurched away from Grace, who sat, frozen, on the ground. The handcuffs fell aside in a faint clatter.

"I called the police," Esperanza said. Her voice shaky, a gurgling noise raising from the back of her throat. "You…you go away."

"I know," he chuckled. "I am the police."

"No," Esperanza breathed. But Grace knew Esperanza had wondered why her mother's murder was never solved, nor was her lover's. The best way was to bury any evidence.

And he must have done so. For one or both of them.

"You killed them," Esperanza screamed. "You vile—"

"Shut your mouth, woman," the man bellowed back, plowing

into Esperanza with his fist. Grace struggled forward. She began to half-drag, half-crawl toward the steps. Her body ached. She was tired, so tired. The man continued to spew invective at her mother, causing Grace to cringe.

She was at the top of the stairs. Freedom.

Her mother screamed.

Grace turned back, desperate to help.

"Run," Esperanza yelled, her eyes meeting Grace's. Run, she mouthed as she dove forward, grappling with the pistol in his hand.

Another blast from the gun. A soft thunk as a body hit the ground.

Grace scrambled forward, her legs shaky, and began to run toward the tree line.

A bullet hit a nearby tree, and Grace ducked, nearly passing out from the pain in her side. She stumbled on.

"Good luck running," he bellowed. "I'll find you. I'll kill you. You'll pay. Oh, you will pay."

Hand clasped to her broken ribs, Grace continued to let those words loop through her mind. Isabel was safe with a father who loved her. Isabel would be safe.

Becky saved her baby. Isabel was safe. Grace had to believe that. Becky knew the law, knew where to take the baby, how to protect her from the monster.

Isabel was safe.

If she wasn't…

Grace hobbled forward, ducking between the boulders and pine trees dotting the property. She knew this place. Her grandfather's property backed up to it. She'd played in these woods often as a child.

Grace had one chance—one place he might not find her. If she could get that far…she bit her cheek to keep from sobbing because that movement made her side hurt worse.

He'd shot her mother.

She glanced back, hoping to catch a glance of the murderer. All she saw was a dark, old-looking SUV near the entrance to the cellar.

Grace gasped, half-sobbing, praying she remembered the location of the cavern. One chance.

She had one chance…

31

Sam

Laws are always useful to those who possess and vexatious to those who have nothing. — Rousseau

Sam dove to the ground a moment before another report from the gun exploded through the forest. Sam tucked his body and rolled behind the boulder, ignoring the small rocks, pine needles and other debris that poked through his shirt and into his skin.

For one moment, Sam's mind caught on the character Edgar in *The Tragedy of King Lear* where the man pretended to be a beggar and shoved rosemary into his skin. Sam never needed the firsthand experience to know that would hurt. And what a time to imagine himself as a Shakespearean hero.

He pulled his gun from its holster. He peeked around the side of the boulder but ducked back quickly as a shot slammed into the rock, pinging off to the left.

Sam rose and fired a shot.

The return was quick. He took a second to scan the area. A ravine that lay to the east. That might be his best opportunity for cover and a semblance of safety.

Sam squeezed off another couple of rounds in an attempt to buy himself some time. His ears rang from the deafening boom of the pistol's discharge. He ducked behind the rock again. There was no return fire. He looked over the edge of the rock. Okay. Now.

He bit his tongue to keep from crying at the pain emanating from his leg up through his torso and into his chest as he sprinted toward the ravine. He breathed deep and focused on the terrain, on his feet, on moving, to keep from blacking out.

Sure, he was woozy from the likely concussion. His vision blurred, making marksmanship difficult. Worse yet, the shooter understood rules of engagement because each shot came from a different location.

In Sam's muddled mind, the shooter appeared to be moving away from him. Which made no sense.

He was safer here, but also easier to pick off should he attempt to pop out of the ravine.

Finally, he heard a sound that made his chest ease.

Sirens.

Coming toward them. Relief swept through him.

In the next moment, he fell flat on his back, agony lancing through his shoulder, stealing his breath…his consciousness.

32

Cici

Liberty may be gained, but can never be recovered.
— Rousseau

Cici woke to an aching head and puffy eyes the next morning. She lunged over and grabbed her phone. Nothing from Sam, but it was already after eight.

Cici yelped as she hopped up from the couch, cringing as a multitude of aches and pains made themselves known. She called the dogs and let them out. She dialed Sam's number. Again, it went straight to voicemail.

Her worry soared into panic.

Unfortunately, she had to be at the church by nine and she wanted to attend Henry's hearing at ten. Sam would have to wait.

Hopefully, he could.

Grabbing the dog's leashes, she got them in her car and sped home. She hopped in the shower just long enough to scrub herself pink before racing to her closet for clean clothes.

Still buttoning her blouse, Cici dashed around her kitchen, prepping the dogs' food and water bowls before she grabbed her purse and a banana and ran out her door.

She arrived at the church at five minutes to nine. The doors were unlocked. Cici entered the administrative offices with caution. The lights were on in her office as well as the main reception area. The smell of coffee perfumed the space.

"So you finally decided to start your day, eh?"

Cici screamed.

Mrs. Sanchez clucked. "My old ears can't take that kind of racket, Reverend. And what's got you in such a lather?"

Cici pressed her hand to her chest, trying to breathe past the vise grip slowly releasing from her chest.

"You scared me," Cici panted.

"I told you I'd come in and sort all this out. Juanito dropped me on the way to work. He's such a good boy."

A different tune from the one she'd sung a month or so ago, but Cici wasn't going to mention it.

Mrs. Sanchez thrust a cup of coffee into Cici's hand. "You look like you need this. It's café con leche. Sit. Drink. Tell me what else needs doing."

In a daze, Cici took her chair. "Else?" she asked.

"Well, I already went over the newsletter and I made some notes on the sermon you left. I don't want to hear that Proverbs quote again. You go to Romans or even Corinthians, but no more of Solomon this week. I made suggestions."

Of course she had. Cici sipped her coffee. She needed it. And a whole other pot. "I'll look it over," she said, trying to be diplomatic. "Um, do you think you can let the mom's group in at nine? Jenny Reid is running the class today. I'd like to go to the custody hearing for Henry and his daughter. It starts at ten."

Mrs. Sanchez shooed Cici back out of her office and the

building. Cici stood in the parking lot again, just ten minutes after she'd gotten there. At least she had a fresh cup of coffee in her hand.

Cici climbed back into her car and headed north toward the old PERA building and to the child custody hearing. She arrived in the parking lot of the corner of Paseo de Peralta and Old Santa Fe Trail with about ten minutes to spare. After looping through the lot only to be forced to turn around twice, thanks to cement barriers, Cici parked and made her way up the front steps toward the majestic white columns. Built in the 30s, this edifice was one of the tallest in Santa Fe. She came in on level three and went to the elevator, pressing the down arrow. Sipping her coffee, she glanced around at the pale marble-tiled walls.

Henry and his lawyer walked in just as the elevator dinged. Cici stepped on and held the door.

"Hello, Henry. Hi, Shawn."

Shawn greeted her warmly whereas Henry dipped his head, his eyes narrowed. Oh, right. She'd run out of his house the other day without explanation.

She waited for the elevator to open to the second floor. The three of them walked toward the Apodaca Meeting room.

"May I speak to you?" Cici asked Henry.

He stopped walking and crossed his arms over his thick chest.

"I'm sorry, Henry," Cici said, her voice filled with contrition. "I…" How to explain? "Becky saw Grace. Before Isabel disappeared." Okay, that didn't sound too strange. "Becky thought you hit Grace."

"Why?" The word carried a deep lament, and another wave of

shame washed over Cici.

"Because Grace had a bruise on her face that day."

"When?" Henry demanded, his jaw tight. "I've never…I would never…I love my wife, Reverend. I…" His voice cracked but he held it together, pushing the gas harder. "If someone hit her, I need to know. I need to protect her."

"I think," Cici said slowly. "I think it was her grandfather. Because Grace wouldn't stop delving into her grandmother's murder."

Fred Ahtone feared for Grace's safety—Cici knew this now from being inside Grace's head. Granted, Fred had lashed out and hurt Grace, which was wrong.

"What do you know about that?" Cici asked.

"I know she died. So did her dad. Years ago. I guess she and Becky had a cousin or aunt or something go missing."

"When was that?" Cici asked.

Henry shrugged. "Um. I don't know. A long time ago, I guess. The cops didn't do much. Grace says they never do."

No one cares what happens to native women, Reverend.

The IAIA artist Sylvia said as much at the MMIW event. Her words reverberated through Cici's head.

What was it about those words she was supposed to recognize?

Want to help me out, Aci?

Unfortunately, her head remained quiet.

"I think their looking into the murders of those women was the catalyst," Cici murmured.

Yes, the certainty grew as she said it.

"Why take Isabel?" Henry asked. "And why did Grace run

away?"

"She didn't," Cici said. She exhaled sharply. "Not like you think."

Shawn stuck his head out the door that led into the stadium-seating amphitheater.

"It's time."

———

Sam still hadn't called by the time Henry was awarded full custody of Isabel. Yolanda Fein came to the hearing, bearing a written statement from Sam that neither CYFD nor the SFPD had reason to believe Henry abused his daughter.

"When did you receive Sam's statement?" Cici asked Yolanda.

"Yesterday." She looked around, frowning. "I thought he was planning to attend."

Cici's stomach burned with worry. "Me, too."

Henry and Shawn joined Yolanda and Cici. They walked toward the elevators.

"Congratulations," Cici said, and Yolanda echoed.

"Thanks. I can't wait to hold Izzy again." Henry smiled and the joy from it beamed over the four of them. Yolanda excused herself to call the emergency foster family and let them know the outcome. Shawn also excused himself, heading toward the elevator.

"What did you mean? About Grace? Earlier," Henry asked.

"About Grace?" Cici asked, distracted by her phone. Still nothing from Sam. She shoved it back into her bag, even as she willed it to ring.

It remained silent.

"I…" Cici paused. She wondered what to say. And how to say

it. "I think Grace got a text from the man who'd killed her grandmother." Sam would have to solve that portion of the case.

"You mean while we were at the police station?"

"Yes. I think she was told to come out to…" Cici paused, needing to remember the route. "705," she blurted. "Route 705. She told me, back in the beginning," Cici mumbled. But Cici hadn't remembered that detail. Damn. She could have had Sam search there days ago. Before Becky died. The guilt ate at her chest, causing her heart to pound. "She went out there to be with Isabel. To try and save her."

"But there's nothing out that way. Maybe a couple of old cabins. For hunting."

Grace hadn't been in the cabin, but Cici didn't want to tell Henry that.

"But then how did Izzy end up back in Santa Fe. And without Grace?"

"Becky," Cici said. "Grace forwarded her the message."

"What message?" Henry asked. He took off his suit jacket and loosened his tie.

"The one from the man." Now, it was all coming back. All the pieces. "The man who killed Grace's grandmother. Her mother."

Henry's gaze lifted to Cici's. His pale eyes opened wide with horror. "Esperanza's dead?" Henry asked, surprise widening his eyes even farther. "And you think Grace is with the man who killed those other women?"

Cici nodded, miserable because that man was running around, hurting people, and Sam hadn't called her back. Sam, who'd gone to Taos without her yesterday.

"Oh, sweet Jesus," Henry breathed. "You said it's on Route 705?" Henry pulled out his phone and pressed some buttons. He pulled up a more detailed topography of Taos. Like a collection of satellite images—crystal clear and lined with coordinates. "Inside or outside the Pueblo?" Henry asked.

Cici closed her eyes, trying to picture the land, what Grace knew of it, what Cici could intuit from her last dream. "I don't know. On the edge."

Henry manipulated his phone some more. "The old Milstead cabin is there, just outside the line."

Cici paled. "You're sure it's Milstead?"

"Yeah," Henry said. "Why?'"

Cici gulped. "Sam said that's the name of the county sheriff."

33

Sam

All wickedness comes from weakness. — *Rousseau*

Sam didn't remember the ambulance ride, though he heard someone talking about his busted knee, blow to the head and some blood loss from his nicked shoulder. He awoke in the Taos Emergency Room.

He swung his legs over the side of the bed. His clothes had been removed and he wore a pair of starchy blue scrubs.

John strode into the room. "Thought you were going to sleep the rest of the investigation away," he said.

"What time is it?" Sam asked.

"About ten."

"In the morning?" Sam asked, voice rising.

Kent stalked into the space. "Good. You're finally awake. How's the arm?"

"Hurts. So does my knee." Sam's lips flipped on with wry humor. "But I'll live."

"Good thing."

"Glad the bullet was a ricochet," Sam said. "Can you imagine if the person managed to get me, point blank?"

"You'd be dead," John said. His hands were in the pockets of his fresh blue jeans, his hair damp at the graying temples from a recent shower.

"We handled the paperwork since you were out," John said. "Figured I'd make sure you got a meal and a shower, too, seeing as how you're still covered in the unfortunate aftermath of last night."

"Any word on what went down?" Sam asked.

John pursed his lips. "We got lots of words. None of 'em particularly helpful. Or kind."

"Why's that?"

"Well, for one, Phil's not cooperating. He decided your attacker was Fred Ahtone. He's out searching for the man now, last I heard," John said with a scowl.

"You two don't get along," Sam said.

John shook his head. "Never liked the man. He's been there over forty years. Everything runs through him."

"How's that different from your department?" Kent asked.

John's lips curved. "Touché. Except I got three deputies I trust with my life. They hauled Sam out of the ravine all right last night."

"Speaking of, can I grab a shower and some coffee? I want to move on the Missing and Murdered Indigenous Women angle."

"We're on it already," Kent said. "Tell us what you know, then you can shower in the doctor's lounge and we'll catch you up to speed."

———

Sam took a shower and changed into the clean clothes John provided. When he limped out of the bathroom, he found John and Kent waiting for him at a small table.

"We have a problem," Kent said.

"Tell me something we don't know."

"The SUV you identified last night is now a burning heap of scrap metal," John said.

Sam muttered a curse.

"Gets worse," John said.

Sam set the cup of coffee Kent handed him on the table with care, trying to find a more comfortable position in the light-ly-padded chair he'd settled himself in.

"And that is?" Sam asked.

"The vehicle's owner is Fred Ahtone. And, according to Phil, the old buzzard is missing."

"All right." Sam wasn't overly surprised by these revelations because they were in line with other criminal activity he'd seen in the past. "So we put out an APB on Fred Ahtone."

"Done," Kent said.

"I got my guys looking for him," John added. "But that's not the problem," he said. He glanced over at Kent, who scowled. The anger in his eyes made him look older, more dangerous.

"The real problem is no one can get in touch with Phil Hartman."

34

Cici

There is peace in dungeons, but is that enough to make dungeons desirable? — Rousseau

---

As Henry's car shot out of the pass and the road settled in alongside the Rio Grande, Cici blurted, "Maybe we shouldn't go."

Henry turned to look at her, a deep frown forming between his eyebrows. "Why? I thought you wanted to check on Detective Chastain."

"I don't…" How to explain that nasty gut feeling—the one that seemed to form before something bad happened—to Henry? "I'm just worried Grace could be in trouble…" Cici grabbed on to the side handle of the sedan as Henry pushed on the gas, zipping past other cars on the highway.

"Look, Reverend, I don't claim to understand what's going on. Last time I saw you, you looked at me like I beat my wife and planned to start pummeling you, too."

Cici gasped. "No, I don't think that, Henry."

"And now you think my wife is alive but injured and needs help. I'm going. If you want me to drop you off, that's fine. But I'm going to the Milstead place right now."

Cici sent yet another text to Sam. It was the tenth of the

morning.

Getting close to Taos. Henry wants to go straight to the old Milstead cabin. If I'm right, there's an old root cellar behind it. Meet us there? Hope you're okay.

She held her phone and her breath, but Sam didn't reply.

Henry continued to push his SUV, and Cici had to put her phone down to grip the side handle once more. Cici sighed in relief when they turned onto the service road. At least the journey was close to an end. Henry bounced them over the terrain with little regard for his struts. He turned into the rutted drive that showed little use and headed toward the house.

It wasn't much of one. More of an old cabin—clearly not consistently lived in.

"Places like these are mostly hunting cabins nowadays," Henry said. "People get a license to shoot elk, deer, bear, whatever and then come out here to stay nearer the animals."

Cici camped as a child, but she shivered at the idea of sitting in this rickety-looking cabin, just waiting for the light to get bright enough so she could shoot an animal. Nope, not ever going to be on her Saturday morning list of fun.

Henry slowed and Cici directed him back farther to where she thought the root cellar would be.

She exited the car on wobbly legs, thankful to be back on stable ground. As she walked back into the scant trees, the wind picked up, sliding over her face and neck. She glanced around, almost expecting to see her sister.

No one stood in the forest. But the wind picked up, all but shoving Cici deeper into the woods. The more steps she took, the harder the wind blew.

Aci was trying to show her where Grace was.

"What are you doing?" Henry asked.

Cici didn't try to explain. She just moved steadily forward, taking the path—best she could—that Grace had taken the night before.

She could almost hear Anna Carmen urging her forward. Almost. Henry kept pace, his long legs eating up the distance much better than hers.

Each time Henry spoke, Cici ignored him, focusing instead on the breeze and her gut. Then, as suddenly as it started, the wind stopped. The air stilled completely, even the birds.

"Here," she said.

"Where?" Henry asked as his gaze darted around.

Cici inched closer. The wall of rock in front of her appeared solid.

A faint waft of stale air hit Cici's nose, causing it to crinkle. Underlying that was a hint of desperation and the metallic scent of blood. She fell forward, yelping in surprise. That wasn't a shadow, it was a narrow crease in the rock, barely big enough for her to fit through.

Henry called her name.

But Cici didn't reply. Instead, she bent down toward the crumpled form lying a few feet in front of her.

Grace lay on her side, her knees pulled up tight to her chest, her hands tucked between her knees. Cici had slept like that on nights when her sister had insisted on keeping the window open in late fall. On nights Cici had worried she'd freeze before morning.

She heard Henry call her name again.

"I'm all right," she muttered.

She couldn't worry about Henry right now. She focused instead on Grace. She gripped the younger woman's arm, shocked by the coolness of her skin.

A pulse. Faint as the breath escaping through her dried, cracked lips. Her skin was bruised, her long, dark hair a tangle of dirt and twigs—maybe dried blood.

Cici settled on her knees next to Grace's head.

"Grace?" she asked.

A faint keen rose from the woman's throat but she didn't open her eyes.

"Grace?" Cici called again, more sharply.

"Isabel…"

The faintest of breaths, but that single word confirmed that Cici stared down at Grace Bruin, beaten, bruised and semiconscious.

"Yes, Grace. She's fine. Safe. I saw her."

Cici's words slowed as she wondered what else to tell the woman struggling for breath on the ground.

"Hang in there," Cici murmured. "So you can see her, too. Soon. You'll get to see her again. Hold your sweet baby. She loves to cuddle. You know that. You can do that, snuggle her. Very soon."

Something rumbled and pinged outside the rock face.

"Henry," Cici called, scrambling to her feet.

More pinging.

Cici nearly sank to her knees. Shots. She'd left Henry out

there, unprotected.

The man who killed Becky was a police officer—she'd neglected to mention that to Henry, too.

Oh, dear Lord. She'd just led both Henry, Grace, and herself into a trap.

35

Cici

If force compels obedience, there is no need to
invoke a duty to obey, and if force ceases to compel
obedience, there is no longer any obligation.
— *Rousseau*

Much as Cici wanted to call out to Henry again, to make sure
he was safe, she worried about drawing the shooter's attention
to Grace's makeshift haven. Cici glanced back at Grace, worry
churning through her stomach and sinking her banana-and-
coffee breakfast low in her guts.

Grace still hadn't regained full consciousness, and her skin was
too cool. Cici worried about exposure to the elements; she didn't
have any of her search-and-rescue gear to even warm Grace up or
offer her some water. She stripped off her silk-and-lace cardigan
and laid it over Grace's supine form, cursing herself for wearing
the matching silk shell. Granted, she'd thought she was going to a
child custody hearing, not traipsing through the woods in pumps
and her best pair of dress pants.

Unwilling to leave Grace alone, Cici stared at the narrow
entrance for a long moment, willing Henry to return. He didn't.

The shooter must have seen Cici fall inside the cavern, which made both Cici and Grace easy pickings for when he came back. The space might be tall, but the floor was narrow and cramped, offering nowhere to hide. Cici patted Grace's hands and murmured, "I'll be right back."

She edged nearer to the entrance. Now she could hear the bullets. They seemed closer, but the reverberations in the cavern made pinpointing an external location impossible. Cici searched the floor and found a decent-sized rock with a sharp edge as well as a rounded bit that fit well in her hand. She leaned her shoulder against the wall, holding her rock.

No, it wasn't much good against a gun, but it was all Cici had. And she intended to use it—especially if the man who'd attacked Grace in her dream showed up here, in this space.

Long, painful moments slid passed. More gunshots ricocheted outside, causing Cici to jump. She stood as near to the opening as she dared. Much as she wanted to peek out to ascertain the growing distance between this cave and the bullets, Cici glanced back at Grace, torn as to whether to return to sit with her or stand guard. Grace's ashen face and faint shivers worried Cici. Just as she'd made the decision to try and share her body heat, voices called back and forth, just outside the rock where she stood.

She leaned in closer to the narrow opening. Cici's heart hammered when she thought she heard Sam's voice. But that could have been due to the strange acoustics in the narrow, tall cave. Cici spoke one of her favorite prayers from the Book of Luke—the doctor, the healer—in a soft, steady tone.

Her legs cramped and her hand ached from being fisted around the rock.

Grace made another low, thick, painful sound in her throat. The woman's shivering subsided. Uh oh, that was a bad sign. From her search-and-rescue training Cici knew shivering meant the body was trying to keep itself warm enough; the lack of muscle fight denoted a lessening of ability to continue to preserve the entire human form.

No help for it. Sharing body heat wouldn't solve Grace's steady deterioration now. Cici gulped a breath and set her rock down. She began to shimmy back through the narrow gap just as a large, tanned hand landed on her arm.

36

Sam

Hatred, as well as love, renders its votaries
credulous. — Rousseau

"I need to check my messages," Sam said.

"Sure," John said. "Let's go by my office. You can charge your phone and get on a computer there."

Sam refused the crutches. His knee was swollen, tender, but the doctor said nothing was permanently damaged or broken. Plus, crutches were a pain to maneuver on. At the doctor's insistence, Sam took the brace but didn't put it on.

At John's office, he plugged his phone into the power cord Brenda lent him. His phone needed a few minutes to charge enough to power up the battery and give him access to his email, contacts, and texts.

Sam sat down at one of the unoccupied computers on a desk nearest John's office while Kent took another. He pulled up his email and clicked on the one from the forensics lab. After reading the scant message, he dialed the direct number he'd been given, using the phone on the desk.

"This is Detective Chastain. I'm calling for…" He checked his screen. "Callie Newman regarding some evidence."

He waited, listening to the terrible music, until a soft voice said, "Hello?"

"Callie? This is Detective Chastain. I got a message stating you had some information for me?"

"Yes, Detective. We didn't get any prints off the keys, purse, or inhaler, but we did find some notches scratched into the inhaler—around that writing. Do you recall that?"

"Yeah. 705 CIV."

"That's what it looks like in pen, but under our microscope, we saw the actual letters were C-a-b-i-n."

"She wrote cabin on her inhaler?"

"Appears so. We're working on the phone. We've tried the passwords provided by the family and thus far, we haven't had much success. But we'll keep trying."

"Great, thanks," he said before hanging up.

Sam leaned back in his chair, staring at the letter. Cabin. As in, go to a cabin? He checked his email again just as his phone's screen lit up. Great. He'd call Cici. She had to be worried.

"705 Cabin," John said.

Sam started. He hadn't heard the other man approach.

"You got any ideas what that could be?" Sam asked.

John's face shifted to a deep scowl. "Yeah. Route 705. I own a cabin back there—edge of the county and tribal lands. I don't use it much but I lease it out to hunters."

"It was on Becky's inhaler."

"Let's go," John said. "Kent! Got us a place to look for Fred."

The ping of multiple incoming texts caused Sam to look down.

"Oh, shit," he breathed.

"What's wrong?"

"Cici's there—at your cabin," Sam muttered.

"How would she know to go there?"

Sam opened his voice mail and pressed "Play" on the messages from Cici. He listened to all five of her messages, scrawling the occasional note. John and Kent leaned forward over his desk, watching him write out the important details.

"She said it's police?" John asked. His mouth turned down and he cursed. "We need more backup, and I don't know who to trust."

Kent stood and picked up his phone. "I gotcha covered."

"What does he mean?" John asked Sam.

Sam's heart beat too fast. Police. Older man. Nice shoes. That's what Gary the vagrant said about the killer. Phil heard them talking last night—heard Sam's theories on the Missing and Murdered Indigenous Women. Phil wasn't here, hadn't been at the hospital.

"When was the last time either of you saw Phil?" Sam asked.

Dawning and immediate fear crested John's face. "I haven't seen him since we were up at Esperanza Ahtone's place. But I spoke with him about the time you were run off the road."

Kent raised his eyebrows. "And almost blown to bits with the vehicle owned by a man we can't find, and thus, can't question."

Police.

Phil had been on the police force since the seventies. What had John said? He basically ran the department.

"We fed him our information," Sam said.

If Phil found Cici…He already knew about her, too. Sam had told him.

Sam swallowed down the fear. "We need to get out to that cabin. *Now*."

———

His phone rang.

"Detective Chastain."

"Detective, this is Phil Hartman."

An icy tendril licked around Sam's heart. "How's it going, Phil?"

"Oh, you know. Same old same old. I found Fred Ahtone."

"You did? Where are you? I'll have John and Kent meet you."

"Oh, that won't be necessary. I handled the situation."

"What are you talking about?" Sam asked. He motioned for John to drive faster.

Phil hadn't called to chitchat. He was fishing for information. Sam checked his voice, trying to keep most of the inflection from it.

"That's not the main reason I called. I wanted you to know I discovered where the Bruin kid was held after her abduction."

Sam wanted to clear his throat. The highway finally opened up in front of them. He tried to sound casual. "You did? That's fantastic. I can be up there in…"

"I'll have it all handled by then," Phil said. "I'm on my way to the old Milstead place now."

"Milstead?" Sam asked.

"Yeah. It's on Service Road 705. John Milstead's familiar with the place since he owns it. Henry Bruin and I are meeting your friend, the reverend Cecilia, there now."

Sam's throat clogged when he heard Henry's howl of outrage.

"Don't come, Detective! It's…"

There was a moment of heavy breathing, and Sam heard something that sounded like a scuffle. A thud. Sam had to bite his cheek to not call out for Henry.

He knew. Somehow, Phil discovered the search led back to him. Panic gripped at Sam's guts.

"What do you want, Phil?" Sam asked. "What did you do to Henry?"

Phil chuckled. The sound reminded Sam of heavy-gauge sandpaper over metal. "Just tying up some loose ends. See you when you arrive."

———

John drove the Bronco out of the sheriff's parking lot and toward the service road. "I can't believe that slimy piece of shit used my cabin."

Sam turned toward Kent. "Who'd you call? For backup?"

"My team," Kent said.

"You work on a team of four officers," Sam said. He checked his pistol, clicked off the safety.

"Actually, my team is up to twenty. But I asked for eight."

John swiveled around to look at Kent, who lounged in the back seat. "Who the hell are you, son?"

"Kent Rivera, Special Agent with the FBI's new Missing and Murdered Indigenous Women's Unit."

So much clicked into place for Sam in that moment.

"You knew it was a dirty cop," Sam said.

"Sure did. Just didn't know which department."

John turned up a drive and past the small, wooden cabin and

into the woods to the east. He parked the SUV between a large rock and a few tall pine trees.

"How long until they arrive?" Sam asked.

"They're bringing in the chopper up from Albuquerque, so I'd guess twenty minutes, maybe less."

Bullets slammed into the windshield, shattering it and sending glass flying. Sam ducked.

John lifted his hand off his head, bits of glass sliding from his short buzz cut, his aviator sunglasses shattered.

He threw off the glasses and squinted in the location from where the shooter stood.

"We don't have that long," John yelled back.

37

Sam

The more ingenious our apparatus, the coarser and more unskillful are our senses. — Rousseau

---

"Plan?" John snapped.

Kent's eyes narrowed and his breathing was labored. "Got hit with a bullet or the glass." He motioned to his side, which dripped blood through his grasping finger.

John cursed. Sam caught a faint movement at twelve o'clock; he steadied his pistol and fired. The reverberation through the car made further attempts at communication useless. John dipped his head toward his door and Sam grabbed his handle.

They both leaped from the car, guns raised.

It went to hell immediately. John cried out when the shooter caught his foot. Phil was a smart bastard. Since bullets couldn't punch through the door's thick metal, he aimed low to neutralize the threat. Sam's knee throbbed, but he dove toward the thicket of unknown brush and rolled behind it.

Kent shoved open his door and dropped to the ground in a tactical position, using the truck as cover while he fired his pistol toward Phil. He bought John enough time to scramble out of the way, though Phil kept up a steady stream of fire that kept all three men pinned to their locations. Kent glanced in Sam's direction and made a "go" motion with his hand.

He was the best option at the moment—Kent wanted him to flank Phil and come in behind. Really, it was their only plan unless they could hold Phil off until the FBI unit arrived.

Sam rose, staggered as he crouched, cursing his stupid injury and hobbling around a bush.

He made his way to the left, stepping as cautiously as he could. Still, he almost yelped in surprise when he spied an older man moving low through the brush, carrying an old rifle combat-style. The man slid behind a tree, his moccasin-clad feet noiseless over the scrubby terrain. He caught Sam's eye and dipped his head.

Fred Ahtone slid back into the shadows moving farther left, no doubt in an attempt to give Sam the closer position. Sam sent up a silent thank-you to Anna Carmen and whoever else might be listening.

"Got your woman, Detective Chastain," Phil called. "She and Grace are dead in a cave. Think you can find them before the animals do?"

Sam swallowed down bile. Oh, Cici. *No.* He couldn't think about that. About Cee, hurt, bleeding. One step, then the next. Take out this threat so he could get to Cici. Sam continued his stealthy maneuvering.

"I have enough firepower here to blow this place up. Like I did your Santa Fe police issue and that old hunk of crap Jeep," Phil called again. He fired at John's badly damaged Bronco, aiming for the engine compartment. If he managed to blow the front of the Bronco up, both John and Kent would be hit, and hit hard, with the shrapnel.

"Got Henry right here. He plans to take the rap for all this—don't you Henry? Wife cheating with a lowlife scum here in Taos. Her plans to leave you developed into a botched kidnapping. Once Henry discovered the plan, he went apeshit and killed his wife and the officers who tried to save her." Phil tutted. "Sad end."

Sam eased closer. Henry lay at Phil's feet, blood dripping from a head wound, face ashen.

Jesus. This guy was reprehensible.

"How many women did you kill, Phil?" John called. He'd made it to the trees while Phil talked and reloaded.

"Not enough," Phil called back. "Never enough," he muttered low.

"Becky Gutierrez, for one. There's a vagrant in Santa Fe that can identify you," John called.

"Not for long," Phil muttered. "Come on. Come on." He cursed.

He must have been having trouble loading a new magazine into the gun. Sam raised his pistol. He crouched, wincing at his swollen knee, as he coiled his muscles, preparing for his first, and probably only strike.

"For Sarah and Kimberly!" cried a voice on the other side of Sam. Fred Ahtone charged Phil, rifle forward. He fired off two shots, but they went wide, digging into the bark of the tree behind Phil.

Phil turned toward him and pulled the trigger on his semi-automatic. Sam couldn't count the number of shots, but they were accurate. Fred slowed, stopped and began to topple forward, blood blossoming across his chest.

Sam took his chance. He leaped forward, pistol held out and firm in both hands. One. Wide.

Two. Better. Shoulder.

Three. Lower. In the side as Phil turned toward him.

Four. Wide. Sam cursed. He'd overcorrected.

Five. Thigh. Though, Sam worried he'd barely clipped Phil with the last shot.

He dropped into the shrubs and rolled again, trying to get out of the line of fire of the weapon that could spray multiple bullets in less than a second.

The sound of pistols and even the AR-15 seemed muffled to Sam's ears as he continued to roll. He ended up behind a tree and checked his clip. Three more in this one. One more clip in his pocket.

Shit. He'd needed to hit Phil better. Because of his miss, they might all die out here.

"Sam!" He looked around the tree.

Henry rose over Phil with a huge roar, not unlike a wounded grizzly Sam had seen as a kid. The big man slammed both fists into the back of Phil's neck. He crumpled.

So did Henry.

Sam stood and began to limp toward Phil and Henry, gun trained on the older man. He lay face down in the dirt. His shirt was riddled with holes, dirt, blood and bits of pine sap.

Sam lowered himself into a crouch, gun still aimed at Phil. He shoved away the man's weapon and rolled him over.

Sightless eyes stared back.

Sam's ears started to clear.

"Sam!"

He turned toward the voice.

Kent staggered his way, swaying like a drunkard. "He down?"

"Dead," Sam said.

John crawled out of his spot fifteen feet from the Bronco, talking into the radio clipped to his shoulder. "Repeat, shots fired. Active gunman neutralized. Multiple injuries. Send ambulance. We need..." He huffed out an almost sob.

Sam sympathized. This shit was serious. Deadly.

Horrifying.

"We need at least three."

"Got it," Brenda's voice called back through the tiny speaker. "Johnny, are you..."

"I'm hit, too, in the goddamn toe." He scowled. "I'll live."

"Thank God." Even Sam heard the relief in her voice. "I have the ambulance coming. One was out on a call. I got you two dispatched and another scrambled. I love you."

John lay against the tire of his destroyed Bronco and sighed. "Love you, too, babe."

John looked up. "Fucking chopper's here."

Kent groaned. John started to laugh.

Sam bent over Henry.

"Where's Cici?" Sam asked as soon as Henry opened his eyes. They were unfocused, but he seemed in better shape than Sam originally suspected.

"Cici, man. Where is she?" Sam asked again, his voice more urgent.

38

Cici

MAN is born free; and everywhere he is in chains.
One thinks himself the master of others, and still
remains a greater slave than they. — Rousseau

Cici screamed.

She raised the rock, ready to strike.

"Really?" Sam's voice—dry and unhappy, but still Sam.

Thank goodness. The rock slid from her fingers, landing on the ground near her foot, as her knees went fluid, utterly incapable of holding up her weight. "You scared me," Cici croaked.

"And you might have made me deaf," Sam said as he pulled Cici from the cavern and into his arms. Cici shivered as the fear slowly drained from her body.

"It's safe now," he said.

"I heard so many shots."

"That was the firefight," Sam said.

"Why does that sound nicer in words than it did in reality?"

"Because active shooters are scary."

Cici pulled back and looked him over, noting the sap and pine needles clinging to his clothes and hair. Her heart tripped when she noticed the blood splattering his shirt. None of it seemed to be coming from him—or at least the small red stains weren't growing.

"Are you okay?" she asked.

"Yeah. Busted my knee a little. Got caught with some rock in my arm last night. It was from a ricochet. But, yeah. A lot better than most of the crew."

Cici pressed her cheek to Sam's chest, listening to his heart as she closed her eyes. "Good golly, Sam."

"That might be the sweetest thing you ever said to me," he murmured, his arms tightening further around her.

"Grace needs help," Cici said, glancing back at the narrow, nearly invisible entrance she'd come through.

"I know. Good thing Henry's so capable with directions and landmarks, even with one helluva bad concussion."

"He's okay?"

"Will be."

"Let me get to Grace," Sam said as he settled Cici to the side. He grimaced as he moved forward, making Cici wonder just how badly he'd pulled or torn or broken the bones and tendons in his knee.

"I think she's in shock. Maybe hypothermia," Cici said.

Sam's concerned expression deepened. "John called for backup soon as he could, and we have three ambulances on the way. Maybe they're here now. Got a boatload of FBI agents roaming the woods." Sam scowled. "They showed up after the fight. 'Kay. Let me go in and grab Grace."

Sam started through the opening.

Another man walked up to Cici, and she started with a yelp.

He was clean, dressed in a bullet-proof vest and FBI cap and windbreaker.

"You found a woman in there?" he asked.

Cici nodded.

The man barreled past, cursing the narrowness of the opening but managed to shimmy through.

Long moments passed. Cici's legs ached from standing in the cave, ready to pounce. She found a relatively flat rock and lowered herself there. She blinked away the déjà vu from her last experience—where she was also shot at—on a mountain, followed by sitting on a rock.

Sam came back and settled next to her, eyes focused on the cave's entrance. "He's going to bring her out since he has two working legs."

The FBI agent came into view. He turned back and bent over, shimmying Grace's sagging body out the too-narrow entrance with as much finesse as he could manage.

Once he managed to tug her past the opening, an EMT Cici hadn't seen join them took over Grace's care, pumping oxygen into her lungs and covering her with a metallic emergency blanket.

"You think she'll make it?" Cici asked.

"You finding her gives her a much better shot," Sam said.

———

Cici wrapped Sam's arm around her waist and helped him limp back toward the clearing. They made it back just as Brenda skidded her four-wheel-drive vehicle to a stop and hopped out, nearly tripping over her seatbelt in an effort to get to her husband. He wrapped her in his arms, rocking her back and forth for a long moment. Cici blinked back tears at the sight of such devotion.

Men and women in FBI caps and jackets, sheriff uniforms, Taos Pueblo Police uniforms, and the Taos PD uniforms called to each other from the cabin and root cellar, working together and around each other.

"This is going to take a while to sort out," Sam said.

He steered Cici away from the unmoving forms of Phil and old Fred that still lay at the edge of the tree line. Instead, Sam headed toward John and Kent. John sat on a large boulder and Kent lay on an orange gurney, both looking gaunt but relieved.

"How are you feeling?" Sam asked.

"Like I've got glass in my gut," Kent grunted. "Thanks for saving the day, man."

He held out his hand and Sam shook it with care. Kent still winced, but a smile ghosted his lips. "The boss said he'd heard of your work both in Denver and that last case you broke in Santa Fe." Kent tipped his head. "I'd expect some heavy recruitment."

Cici's gaze flashed up to Sam's face, but he just squeezed her waist.

"Not interested," Sam said.

Kent shrugged, then grimaced. "Not sure that'll matter. You're the superstar here today. Figured out the evidence and brought down the baddie before he took out more civvies. Good work, Detective."

"I'm still mad you didn't tell me you were FBI."

Kent nodded. "I get that a lot."

Sam shook his head. The EMTs hoisted Kent into the back of

the ambulance and slammed the doors shut.

"They already took Henry and Grace to the hospital," John called. "Once they staunch the bleeding here, we'll head on down to the hospital. Brenda'll drive us."

Still pale, Brenda nodded. "I want you to get that looked at better than by a paramedic," she said, her tone between scolding and quavering.

"Yes, ma'am. I plan on it. Hurts like a son-of-a-bitch."

Brenda held his hand while an EMT knelt at his foot, bandaging his bloodied big toe. Sam lifted his sore leg off the ground, leaning more on Cici. She tightened her grip and sighed with relief.

"I'll get my knee looked at, too. I think I should've taken the doc up on that brace or those crutches," Sam said with a wince.

Finally, the four of them shuffled to the car, Brenda and Cici helping the men hobble over.

"We need to hire more emergency personnel," John grumbled.

"That would mean we plan on having more of these types of incidents," Brenda shot back.

"Good point," John said with a sigh as he settled into the front passenger seat. He glanced back at Sam and Cici. "Are your cases always this full of gunshots and adrenaline?"

"Thankfully, no," Sam said. "Just the ones that Cici's involved with."

Much as Cici wanted to dispute this claim, she couldn't. Mainly because she'd only been involved in two now and in both, bullets flew.

Cici no longer wondered if her sister somehow remained on

Earth, somehow nearby—she must. Yeah, her sister was helping her solve crimes.

Two in less than three months is a pretty fast clip, Aci.

———

John and Sam finally saw their respective doctors about the time Henry woke up. Cici sat with him for a while, promising to make sure Isabel remained safe with her foster mom until Henry could pick her up. She contacted Yolanda to let her know the details. She handed her phone to Henry so he could hear Yolanda reiterating Cici's promise to take good care of Isabel.

Cici returned to the waiting room to find Brenda sprawled out in a chair. "John was struggling to maintain his tough-man demeanor while they poked at his toe. I figured I'd come out here so he could whine like he wants to."

"Will his foot be okay?" Cici asked.

Brenda nodded. "So the doctor tells me." She looked down. "I'm so sorry to hear about Becky." She shifted her gaze back up toward Cici, her eyes wide and filled with sorrow. "Gemma's a good friend of ours. Her daughter Beck went to school with our youngest."

Cici licked her lips, but she remained at a loss as to what to say or how to help.

Brenda leaned back in her chair. "At least it's over. Thank God this nightmare is over."

EPILOGUE
Cici

I do not know the art of being clear to those who do not want to be attentive. — Rousseau

"That was a beautiful service," Sam said. He wrapped an arm around Cici's shoulders and squeezed.

Cici glanced up at him, squinting against the sun's glare. "I hope Becky liked it. I wasn't sure…"

Becky's mother waddled over. The tiny woman's face was lined in wrinkles. The small white lines at the corners of her eyes told of a life of laughter but the thick grooves around her mouth came from too much sorrow.

"Mrs. Gutierrez." Cici took the older woman's hand between both of hers, holding the soft, if papery skin for a long moment, trying to imbue some sense of calm—or at least caring.

"That was a nice service, Reverend Gurule. Thank you for saying some kind words about my daughter. I know she and Grace think very well of you."

"Of course."

"Not of course. You have to be wanting your own bed, but I've found it's important to get the rituals handled quickly. That way we can mourn our loved ones. I've been to too many funerals."

Too many, Cici averred in her head.

"Becky would have liked it. Especially knowing baby Isabel is back with her father as she belongs."

"I wish I hadn't had to give a eulogy for her," Cici said on a sigh. "She deserved more time. More life."

"Ah, but you and I both know it is not about time, Reverend. Me, I have had time. Many years." Mrs. Gutierrez's voice turned querulous. "I've buried my parents, my husband, my sisters and brothers, and now even one of my children." Her gray curls fluttered when she shook her head. "These years have brought so much sorrow."

Cici held the older woman's hands for a moment longer, trying to transfer some strength. "If there's anything I can do to help, you just call me."

Mrs. Gutierrez's rheumy eyes smiled up into hers. "I'll keep that in mind, young lady. Maybe you come to visit this old woman sometime."

She patted Cici's cheek and moved off, calling to her son to come take her arm.

"Phil Hartman was a sick sack of crap," Cici said, leaning against Sam's shoulder. He brought his hand up and stroked her hair.

"Yes, he was. Best we can tell, he killed about fifteen women over the course of his career. Grace's grandmother and great-aunt were two of his victims. So was Grace's father. He had a real thing for that family."

"How much more investigating needs to happen?" Cici asked.

"A lot." Sam squinted into the sun. "When I was over at

the sheriff's department earlier, John told me the FBI wants to exhume a greater area around John's cabin. He told the FBI to do whatever they needed to do."

"He's a good man," Cici murmured. He'd come to Becky's funeral in a wheelchair, but Brenda had already taken him back to the office. The Taos criminal justice departments were reeling from the most recent murders—and the fact one of their own was the culprit. John told both Cici and Sam before the service that he refused to take time away from his office until all the necessary details were handled.

"He likes you, too. And Brenda's singing your praises. I heard she wants you to meet her oldest son."

Cici rolled her eyes even as a blush stained her cheeks. Being set up on dates made Cici uncomfortable, which gave Sam greater ammunition. He smirked.

"We need to talk," he said, his voice turning solemn.

Oh, no. No, they did not need to talk about that kiss weeks ago. Not if Sam regretted it, as he'd said a few days before.

Before Cici managed to work out an escape plan, Henry ran over, Isabel tucked against his side like a football. "Reverend!" he cried.

He had a bandage over his forehead from a bullet, and his face was splotchy from the cuts and nicks he experienced while Phil Hartman dragged him through the brush, but his grin was huge. Isabel kicked her feet and squealed, no doubt pleased with the bumpy ride to get to Cici's side. Henry puffed out a breath.

"She's going to be okay," he gasped.

"Who?" Sam asked.

"Grace." Henry nearly bounced with happiness.

"I'm so glad for you, Henry." Cici smiled. "And, you, too, Isabel."

"I'm heading back over to the hospital now," Henry said. "To the hospital. I was there all last night until the funeral today. Yolanda just brought me Izzy. I'm so glad because now I can take her to see her mama. Grace has missed her, so much. I'm glad she's with us again."

Henry's smile turned solemn. "But Grace…she's real upset about Becky." Henry cleared his throat. "She's still dehydrated and bad-hurt, that's why she wasn't here today even though she begged. The doctor said she needs to rest. But I'll get her fixed up." Henry beamed, his eyes wet with tears of joy and pain. Like so much of these last few days, those emotions tended to mingle too easily.

Sam stepped forward and offered Henry his hand. Henry stared at it for a moment before extending his own.

"I was wrong not to trust Cici's judgment. She saw the love you have for your family. Your loyalty and dedication to them. I can't tell you how happy I am you're getting this opportunity for happiness after these past weeks of pain and disappointment."

Henry's tears spilled over, but that didn't stop him from pumping Sam's hand with enthusiasm.

"Thanks, man," Henry said. He cleared his throat to continue, "That means a lot."

Henry let go of Sam, who winced almost imperceptibly, wiggling his fingers. Cici braced herself for the same enthusiastic onslaught, but Henry enfolded Cici against his chest as gently as he cuddled his daughter.

"Thank you." Henry gulped. "For everything."

He turned and trotted away across the cemetery. Cici tipped her face up to the soft breeze.

"I owe you an apology, Sam. I shouldn't have gotten so angry, pushed you so hard, about wanting to keep Isabel safe." Cici opened her eyes and met his gaze. "That was badly done of me, and I'm deeply sorry to have caused you any hurt."

"I guess we're even then," Sam said. "I was an ass, too."

Cici breathed deep and was thankful. For the sun, for Sam. For Henry's happiness and the love he shared with Grace and Isabel. Though still saddened by Becky's unnecessary death, along with Esperanza and Fred Ahtone.

Cici said a prayer for the brave young woman and the elderly man who'd suffered for so long, who'd willingly sacrificed himself to make sure his wife and daughter's killer was brought to justice.

Esperanza…Cici felt the same ambivalence Grace had experienced toward her mother during Cici's vision in the root cellar. Without Esperanza's sacrifice, Grace would be dead. But the woman abused her child for years.

Cici still struggled with how to tease out that messy set of experiences. She'd called Grace before the service today, and they'd talked some. Cici hoped Grace took her up on the offer to talk more.

Sam limped toward the rental car they'd be taking back to Santa Fe.

"How's the knee?" she asked.

"A bit better today," Sam replied. "I'll take the brace off soon,

I think. Good thing I can drive. You, Cici, have a lead foot."

Cici shrugged, not even trying to deny his accusation. She liked a bit of speed—that's why she liked her motorcycle, too. "Soon we can start hiking again, then," Cici said. "I've missed those days."

"I'd like that," Sam replied.

Before she opened the car door, Cici took one last look around the cemetery. Tree branches swayed in a soft breeze. Birds chittered. The sky was impossibly blue and the sun blazed bright and hot.

Thanks, Aci. I needed this moment. It's grounding. Reminds me to be thankful for what I have.

The breeze danced around Cici, tugging with gentle insistence at her clothes.

Sam turned to look at her. "You misunderstood me the other day," he said.

"You don't need to say anything," Cici said, trying and failing to keep her voice level.

"I do, though. I thought…" He leaned his head back. "Phil said he'd killed you."

Cici reached over and grasped his hand. "Well, he didn't."

Sam squeezed her fingers back. "I'm glad. And, for the record, I don't regret kissing you."

"No?"

Sam shook his head. "I don't regret telling you about my father either."

Cici's smile was watery. "I'm glad you feel okay with trusting me."

He raised his hand to her cheek. "It's never been an issue of trust, Cee. You've had it since the seventh grade."

"Sam," Cici said on a sigh. "You've always been an important part of my life."

His smile was crooked but genuine. "Good. Want to grab some dinner?" Sam asked. "How about a green chile cheeseburger and a milkshake? We'll swing by Shake Foundation once we hit Santa Fe, take it to go if you want."

She hesitated. Not because she didn't want a lavender milkshake—*don't judge until you try it*—but because she was tired and heart sore. Once again, she'd ended up in a family drama that brought up the simmering resentment Cici still held toward her own father. Cici made note to call him. Soon.

"Okay. I'd like that."

"I'll even let you eat in the rental car," Sam wheedled. His light tone helped shift the mood between them. "Won't matter if you spill ketchup on those seats."

Cici stopped walking and looked up with an annoyed huff. "One time, Sam. That happened *once*."

He applied a gentle squeeze to her shoulders. "And I still get to give you shit about it."

She really wanted a lavender milkshake now that the idea floated through her head. "Okay. But I want onion rings."

"Gah," he grumbled. "You know I hate onions. Those things stink."

"Who helped you solve the case, Sam? Who found Grace, hmm? Who helped keep an innocent child out of the hands of a monster?"

Cici pointed her thumb at her chest. "Your secret weapon wants onion rings, Sam-o. And a big-ass shake. Deal with it."

"What reverend says 'ass'?" Sam grumbled. "And onions are gross."

But, Sam being Sam, he dealt. Cici kept the bag tightly sealed until she was seated at her dining table, Sam's leg propped on the chair next to him.

Sam sat across from her while her dogs snoozed on their beds. With a start, Cici realized she could see moments like these playing out for the next forty…maybe even fifty years.

With Sam.

She set her milkshake back on the table, unable to hold it in her shaking hand.

With Sam.

Had Aci known?

Cici didn't understand what was going through her mind. Just that her heart wanted to beat out of her chest.

"I was worried about you, Cee. And I feel like I really should tell you…"

Sam glanced up, midsentence.

Whatever was in Cici's expression caused him to pause speaking. He tilted his head, like he was trying to decipher something an unknown language.

Before he managed to ask a question, Sam's phone rang. Cici gulped in a breath and said a small prayer of thanks. She wasn't sure what she was thinking, not in this moment. And she sure didn't want to articulate her jumbled emotions to Sam.

Sam wiped his hands on a napkin, mouth puckering with

displeasure as he answered.

"Hello, Jeannette."

Cici stilled, her eyes widening. Jeannette. Sam still spoke to his ex-girlfriend?

He hadn't said so before. Granted, they hadn't really been talking much. Then, the whole situation with baby Isabel and Sam's own demons, but how did he not tell her he was talking to his ex-girlfriend?

Then again, why would he?

"So you talked to the FBI head here, huh? Yeah, I know Kent Rivera's been talking me up." Sam was silent for a beat, then he scooted back from the table, shoving his meal back into the bag. "You did what?" Sam barked. "I never asked you to do that," he snapped.

Cici's eyes widened.

Phone still to his ear, he waved, mouthing, *gotta go*.

He limped out.

Cici huffed, annoyed…and yes, hurt. What about *their* talk? What had Sam planned to tell her?

After tossing out their trash, Cici collected her mail and watered her sparse collection of plants. She walked down the hall to her office where she shuffled through her email. Her chest tightened as she clicked on one from an old friend of hers who now worked at a large church outside of Portland.

She skimmed the letter, a very flattering letter, that said the members of the search committee had heard great things about her work. Would she be interested in meeting? They'd love to have her do a phone interview this week, then, if it went according to plan, a visit to the church would be set up for next week.

Cici glanced around her small home office. What, really, was keeping her here, in Santa Fe?

ACKNOWLEDGMENTS

As always, thank you, Chris. Your unwavering support and love shine through in all you do for the kids and me. I couldn't ask for a better man, and I'm thrilled to wake up with you each day. You're also the best movie date a gal could ask for.

To Corinne Jones, who shared her police and criminal justice expertise. Thank you for making sure I wrote correctly about the jurisdictions and Sam's investigation. Getting this right matters to me, and your expertise made this manuscript so much stronger—thank you so, so much.

To my family, thank you for your patience with my dream—and letting me hang out in my head *way* too often.

To my AuthorLab writing pals: You keep me on task and keep me motivated. I love your commitment and passion. I love reading your posts and stories. And I love how diverse our group is.

LERA ladies and gentlemen, thank you for being so supportive, for making me love writing again, and for sharing your knowledge so freely. You are the best.

To Deborah Nemeth, thank you for pushing me to make this story better--for challenging me when and where I needed to be challenged.

To Nicole Pomeroy, thank you for being so detail oriented. I can't tell you how much I enjoy working with you because I know my books are so much better after your edits.

To my Team, who have stuck with me and encourage me and

read all my ARCs as well as whatever quirky thought I decide to share on Facebook. Thank you. I appreciate each of you.

To Emma Rider, this cover is gorgeous. Thank you for sharing so much of your beautiful self in it.

And to my readers and reviewers. I would not be where I am today without you. I cannot thank you enough for sharing your time with me.

ABOUT THE AUTHOR

With a degree in international marketing and a varied career path that includes content management for a web firm, marketing direction for a high-profile sports agency, and a two-year stint with a renowned literary agency, Alexa Padgett has returned to her first love: writing fiction.

Alexa spent a good part of her youth traveling. From Budapest to Belize, Calgary to Coober Pedy, she soaked in the myriad smells, sounds, and feels of these gorgeous places, wishing she could live in them all—at least for a while. And she does in her books.

She lives in New Mexico with her husband, children, and Great Pyrenees pup, Ash. When not writing, schlepping, or volunteering, she can be found in her tiny kitchen, channeling her inner Barefoot Contessa.

The next page is an excerpt of An Artifact of Death,
A Reverend Cici Gurule Mystery Book 3.

1

Cici

"Wheresoever you go, go with all your heart."
— *Confucius*

"Check the perimeter," the guttural voice charged. "Shoot anything that moves."

From bad to worse in a heartbeat. Cici's gaze darted around, looking for a possible place to hide. Boots crunched over the dry ground, as the man stepped ever nearer.

She tipped her head, straining to catch any further words on the heat-soaked breeze. Eighty-nine degrees at her last check in around three in the afternoon. The heat wave and drought refused to break even this late in September, causing unpleasantness for the entire region.

Now, as her heart thumped in arrhythmic sympathy, her mind conjured scenarios for the men.

None of the thoughts were positive.

Footsteps neared. Cici stiffened, each muscle quivering, as one of those voices rose, the pitch loud and full of anger. Hostility dripped from the words. She peeked around the wall where she sat and her heart tripled.

And in that moment, Cici feared not just for her life, but the other two male voices because....because....

He gripped a gun in his fist.

She stared at the dull metal barrel, her bag of trail mix sliding from her fingers, her mind numb.

Cici took a deep breath of dust-clogged air. She stiffened her spine and gave a mental middle finger to the entire world, including her sister.

No way Cici was dying, bleeding out under the harsh New Mexican sun because she was in the wrong place. Out here, in the middle of nowhere—one of the most deserted stretches of desert in the entire country. That's why Cici chose it. To consider her life and plan her future. She wasn't dying before she figured out her future.

No way, Anna Carmen Sandra Gurule.

Wow. Her sister had a long name. She'd never understood her sister's double first name, but Cecilia and Anna Carmen had the same number of syllables, so Cici rarely gave it much thought.

The randomness of her thoughts helped calm her enough to get a deep breath into her lungs. No longer lightheaded, Cici's vision improved and she managed to drag in another breath, ears straining for the next sound—any indication of where the men were.

She'd wanted to weigh the pros and cons of the executive reverend position for the large church in Portland, Oregon. When she flew up and interviewed with the large search committee a few weeks ago, she hadn't expected to be offered the position—not with the quality candidates they'd be assured to bring in.

But the church committee *did* offer Cici the job with a nice salary and a moving package to entice her further. Temptation flitted through her overlaid by disappointment and despair.

She wanted a *life*.

No, she wanted a family. A deep, intimate connection to people within her world. Which meant something in her current life must change—something huge, like her job or the pseudo-communications with her dead twin.

Something big…but not this. Never, ever yet another life-or-death, kill-first-never-bother-to-ask-questions situations.

One of the men said, "Really, is all this drama necessary? I mean, your little oil production is cut off while for a while—"

The guttural voice cut him off.

"Save it. You know why you're out here."

He had a slight accent—one not native to this area. Cici couldn't place it.

"No, I don't, actually," the first man's voice turning almost conversational. "Can't say I expected you to drag me out into the ruins with guns. I mean, that feels very eighties spy novel. Back in the Cold War days."

Who the heck remained conversational—so casual and unperturbed—when someone pointed a gun at them?

Cici never wanted to find out if she was capable of that particular skill. She supposed she should say *again*. She'd had to do that before, the whole time trying not to lose control of her voice or bowels. She did, however, want to point her camera at the man and get a decent picture of Guttural Voice who was threatening the man. She rose slowly from her crouch and tried to hold her phone steady enough to snap a clear picture.

The first time she pressed the button, it made the shutter-click sound. Cici dropped to the ground with a grimace as she flipped the switch to set her phone in silent mode. Her breathing once again faded to ragged.

Lord, she was the worst stealth investigator in the history of the world. Her stomach rippled as she held her breath, all muscles poised to flee.

"What was that?" Guttural Voice asked.

"At no time was kidnapping or murder suggested as part of the plan." The man was on a roll or he'd seen Cici—at least heard her camera click—and tried to distract the bad guy. Was that something she wanted? To be in one of these men's debts?

Could she allow a man to be shot and not try to save him?

Too many thoughts rammed through her brain so quickly, Cici couldn't grasp any of them.

"Check out that noise, Don."

"You said no one was here."

Cici assumed that was Don talking. Not the voice of the other two. Don had a thicker accent than Guttural Voice. Eastern European, maybe?

"I told you to check the perimeter. There's a car here," Don complained.

Cici tensed, having forgotten about the other guy—Don— who was supposed to *kill everything on sight.*

That was not a statement to forget. *Ever.*

Cici edged further away from the voices, intent first to buy herself some distance. Her only option appeared to be a mad sprint back toward her car.

Her car was only about three-tenths of a mile from her current location. Less than half a mile, if she could get around the kivas and haul butt.

She peered out at the flat, barren landscape devoid of trees or even clumps of boulders to hide behind and grumbled another curse. Most of the time Cici loved New Mexico. Today when her life hung in the balance? Not so much.

Chaco Canyon National Park was a group of interconnected, dusty ruins built into the northwestern New Mexico landscape that offered a glimpse into a vast pre-Columbian cultural complex used for ceremonies, trade, and political activity. While interesting enough to garner a UNESCO seal, Cici had been fascinated with the Chacoan society because of a story her mother Sandra told Cici and her sister as they sat overlooking the Plaza in Santa Fe--the last place the gambler was supposed to visit.

Anna Carmen begged their mom to drive them to Chaco, but they'd never had time. Later, once Sandra died, Anna Carmen asked Cici to go with her to poke through the great house built by the Chacoans to buy back the men, women, and children won by the gambler, but Cici had been too far away, then too busy.

Today, she was fulfilling that promise to her sister, poking through Pueblo Bonita, one of the many ruined complexes, taking in the sheer majesty of the multi-storied adobe structure, when the voices drifted forward on the wind.

Now, after seeing the guns, Cici knew, deep in her bones, she had moved well beyond the realm of reasonable and into a previously nonexistent category of most ridiculous set of luck a human could possibly anticipate.

She wished her dogs were with her. Or Sam.

That situation was probably nothing more than a misun-
derstanding--one that caused her to slink from town at the
first opportunity. The problem was, Cici couldn't see Detective
Samuel Chastain and remain pal-around-gal she'd been all these
years. Ever since he kissed her, Cici's lips tingled whenever she so
much as heard his voice. And that was just…just…well, it was
damn uncomfortable was what it was.

Later. Focus on that later. When she wasn't so near guns. Crap
on Challah bread. This wasn't how she saw her first vacay in *three
years* going.

She needed a thick copse of trees to dash into. Or more rocks.
Anything she could hide behind and use to her advantage.

Sadly, nothing appeared.

She sucked in a deep breath and edged toward the doorway.
From it, she looked forward through three more doorways. She
kept her back pressed firmly against the adobe bricks. Mud and
straw—not much protection against a bullet, but the best Cici
could use. Nothing moved.

With a deep breath, she scuttled forward, much like a hermit
crab darting from the safety of one too-small shell to its hopeful
new home.

Out of the corner of her eye, she saw two of the men. The man
pointing the gun seemed more nervous than the man staring down
the barrel. He must have caught her movement from the corner of
his eye because he shifted, forcing Guttural Voice to turn his back
toward Cici as she edged further through the complex.

"Care to explain how we moved from casual acquaintances of maybe-we-should-work-together to you pointing a pistol at my chest?"

At the next intersection, Cici paused. She breathed in deep and let the breath trickle out, seeking enough serenity to think of a plan. Her brain kept screaming *run!*

But that wasn't her smartest move. Not with more than a quarter mile between her and her car—the only route of escape. Keys! They were in her pack. She needed those to make a faster getaway.

Slowly, to avoid making any additional noise. Cici took off her pack and shoved her hand inside the small side compartment. She took her time, undoing the clip that held her key chain with one hand, grasping the keys with her other fist.

"When you decided to stick your nose into our business and take items that do not belong to you."

"Let me play along. Suppose I did take something—and I'm not saying I did. But if I did. Were you the original owner?"

"You say stupid things. Who owned originally doesn't matter. What matters is I have it now."

"But, based on what you just said, you do not have the…what is it?"

Guttural Voice swore. "You're trying to confuse me. Trying to bait me into telling you what I took…" Guttural Voice cursed again. "Never mind that. You didn't do your homework on the Bratva." Guttural Voice seemed to be speaking away from her.

Bratva? Cici shook her head. Not a word she knew.

"I work in permitting oil and gas leases for the State of New

Mexico. Until now, I've never heard anyone mention something called the Bratva," the man said. "Doesn't sound Spanish."

Where was Don? Hopefully moving toward the back of the complex, where Cici stood moments before.

Guttural Voice laughed, but it sounded more like a dying donkey. "Oh, it isn't. But you know what it is. Lesson one, the Bratva does not hand out invitations, Mr…, ah, what did you want us to call you? Right. Vasiliev."

Cici reshouldered her pack into the middle of her back and grasped her keys in her hand.

Russian surname. Cici had heard it often enough in Manhattan and in Boston.

Cici scooched forward, trying to control her breathing as she worked her way around one of the rounded kivas in the floor.

Why the pre-Puebloans chose to build so many sinkholes proved incomprehensible. Yes, yes, the kivas connected the underworld with the earthly realm. This was their church. All great points, but large kivas made escaping the complex more difficult.

Maybe that was the point.

Anna Carmen, I'm sorry I was angry with you. I need some help. Now would be a good time to…do something. Like commune with any shaman or another spirit hanging out here, unhappy to have invaders clambering all over their spiritual sites.

In that brief flash of panicked prayer, Cici never considered herself an unwelcome invader. She swallowed hard. Wait. The Chacoans disappeared hundreds of years before the great Spanish drive north into this part of the country.

Okay…so maybe, to the Chacoans, Cici wasn't a *conquistadora*.

Her family invaded their homelands. She totally was an invader.

Never mind, Aci. I just need help to get out of here.

"Sergei, come here!"

Guttural Voice—his name was Sergei—grumbled.

"What?"

"Found a baggie. It's half full of trail mix."

"So?" Sergei called back.

"Looks new. Chocolate bits aren't that melted. Yum. This is good stuff."

Sergei grumbled about how something could look new when it was litter. He must have moved toward Don. Cici worked her way around the next circle. Nearly back to the path. Her chest tightened. This mad dash would be the scariest part. She would not be able to look back to see if the men were shooting while simultaneously dodging cacti and rocks.

She sucked in a deep belly-full of air, just like she used to be a lacrosse game. Another as she settled into the old, comfortable running position.

Behind her, the sound of scuffling rose.

Pah-ting!

Cici jerked. No, not a firecracker going off. She was too familiar with that sound.

Pah-ting. Pah-ting. Pah-ting. Pah-ting.

Her heart raced as she shoved off the ground and broke into a sprint.

Behind her, more gunshots slammed into the earth.

CPSIA information can be obtained
at www.ICGtesting.com
Printed in the USA
FSHW02n1047231018
53224FS